To

WHO SHOT THE SHERRIFF?

An Original Story

By

PROLIFIC, NATIONAL BESTSELLING AUTHOR

JOHN A. ANDREWS

CREATOR OF

THE RUDE BUAY SERIES

RENEGADE COPS

&

THE WHODUNIT CHRONICLES

06/02/1A

WHO SHOT THE SHERRIFF?

Published in the U.S.A. by
Books That Will Enhance Your Life

A L I
Andrews Leadership International
www.AndrewsLeadershipInternational.com
www.JohnAAndrews.com

ISBN: 978-0-9848980-3-9
Cover Design: ALI
Edited by: Professor Harminder Kaur

THE

WHODUNIT

CHRONICLES

The HUSTLE

The FLOW

The VERDICT...

WHO SHOT *THE* SHERRIFF?

WHO SHOT THE SHERRIFF?

TABLE OF CONTENTS

CHAPTER 1

The luscious green mountainous terrain in the north stretches and recedes towards the low land area golf courses and the elaborate nineteenth century town square houses in the south of the city of Mandeville, Jamaica. Mandeville is the capital city and largest town in the parish of Manchester in the county of Middlesex, Jamaica. In 2005, it boasted a populous of over 50,000, plus at least another 25, 000 including the suburbs. Today, almost a decade later that population has more than doubled.

Situated on an inland plateau, it is the only parish capital of Jamaica not located on the coast or on a major river. Mandeville is sandwiched in Manchester between the parish of Saint Elizabeth to the West and Clarendon to the East. Additionally, it is located approximately 64 miles from Kingston, Jamaica's capital and 65 miles from Montego Bay, another capital city otherwise known as MO' Bay.

The town square, much of an English town setting has a court house, a parish church and clock tower, and many large elegant early nineteenth-century houses which line the winding streets in the town center. The plush green grass adds luster to the setting of the antiquated town square. The blue print for this town, nestled in Jamaica, was laid out in 1816 and named after Viscount Mandeville, the eldest son of the Duke of Manchester, who was then governor of Jamaica.

Many of those original buildings can still be seen, such as the stature of the courthouse, an impressive building of cut limestone with a horseshoe staircase and a raised portico supported by Doric columns and built in 1820. This building, during the week is usually filled with lawyers and their clients. The oldest dwelling in Mandeville is the rectory beside the courthouse, also built in the same year.

WHO SHOT THE SHERRIFF?

IN THE SUBURBS TODAY, many who have struck it rich and returned from North America and the United Kingdom show off their hard work and pizazz by building massive houses. So much that developers keeping up with the trend have complemented these mansions with large housing developments, most of which are expansive gated communities.

It is documented that many of Jamaica's oldest businesses were started in the city of Mandeville; such as the Mandeville Hotel, which began operations in 1875 and the Manchester Golf Club, the first in the Caribbean founded in 1868. Some of the local festivities in Mandeville include the "Manchester fiesta" which is held on August 8. While the South Manchester sweet potato festival is held every year on October 28.

In 1957, the Alcan Bauxite Company in a joint venture with the Jamaican Government gave the city a shot in the arm when it built houses for its then mostly expatriate staff. The relatively high wages lured many educated Jamaicans to Mandeville. Subsequently the town has seen an influx of Jamaicans as well as foreign intellectuals, including lawyers, doctors and other high ranking officials. It is home to the Northern Caribbean University (formerly West Indies College), a Seventh-day Adventist institution of higher learning.

WHO SHOT THE SHERRIFF?

All in all, it's a great place where the neighbors know each other and frequently eavesdrop on each other's affairs.

Some of the notables from Mandeville include: Donovan Bailey, retired Olympic sprinter, Charmaine Crooks, Olympic athlete, Sheryl Lee Ralph, actress and singer, Winston McAnuff, reggae musician, Heavy D (born Dwight Arrington Myers), rapper, Lovel Palmer, Jamaican and international footballer, Garnett Silk, reggae musician and Christopher Williams, an athlete.

In Peter Tosh's version of "Johnny Be Goode", he sings about a hut on the top of a hill which is "Deep down in Jamaica close to Mandeville." While in Bob Marley's "Mr. Brown," the character is noted as being asked for, "from Mandeville to Sligoville." Not to confuse him with "Sheriff John Brown" in *I Shot the Sheriff.*

WAY BEFORE BOB MARLEY, Peter Tosh, Jimmy Cliff, Dennis Brown, Freddie McGregor, Gregory Isaacs, Johnny Nash, John Holt and Eric Donaldson entered the musical era. A college professor and Mandeville native, Sebastian Haynes, born way before the civil rights revolution met and married his wife Megan Williams.

Several years later they gave birth to their first and only son Wesley Haynes at Mandeville hospital. Wesley came in at nine pounds and twenty-two inches. His mom, a nurse in the field of obstetrics and gynecology saw him as the perfect size for a newborn. Mr. and Mrs. Haynes always envisioned themselves as a king and queen even before they said "I do" inside the Mandeville Park.

Now in their eyes years later their little bundle of joy Wesley was their prince, and he would be privy of the inheritance, that of their imaginary throne.

CHAPTER 2

More than a decade later, Megan and Sebastian Haynes watched with much amazement as their son Wesley entered into his teenage years. At thirteen he possessed commanding leadership skills in sports. Wesley Haynes played soccer, cricket, basketball, volleyball and ran track at Manchester high school. He became so adept in track and field that his coach Conrad

Fredricks nominated him for a nation-wide competition.

Unfortunately, Wesley was unable to compete in the tournament for which, he had worked so hard to qualify. Just one month prior to the competition he broke his left leg playing basketball in the neighborhood park. He attended the event but sat there with his leg propped up in a cast. This was tough for the young Haynes, who sat there in limbo watching others compete, while envisioning better days to come.

As his voice deepened, together Megan and Sebastian stayed up late at nights after a hard day's work and sought out colleges and universities that, he could attend and later earn a law degree. The steady influx of lawyers in that fluid community was on an all-time high. You say lawyer and an imaginary bell goes off in the city of Mandeville signaling the welcoming of Manchester's baby boomers.

The local Ad-signs posted in multiple locations said we can help you with legal representation for divorce, accidents, personal injury, malpractice, bankruptcy law, criminal defense, child custody, real estate law, immigration law, drug litigation, DUI and traffic related tickets.

One astute commuter, who meditated on those billboards every morning and evening while in the process of earning his livelihood, years later, had this to say:

WHO SHOT THE SHERRIFF?

"It seemed like the legal industry was cashing in, while law schools were preparing new students for their gold rush."

Back then, whenever Megan and Sebastian, who, focused on developing potential in Wesley, mentioned their goals for their son to the neighbors, those nationals questioned Megan and Sebastian's intention for wanting their son to become what they called a *deep pocket,* a *traitor* and a *jinnile.* They not only felt that the profession was already saturated there in Mandeville but added:

"Lawyers are a bunch of liars, thieves and crooks; they will sue their own mother if they get a chance."

By this time the few bad grapes in the bunch of legal scholars living in Mandeville were noticeable, some of them smelled so bad, it had become a stench.

The number of lawyers not only grew in Mandeville but expanded to other areas of Manchester as well. Even though the city was a breeding ground for higher educational learning, the neighbors saw the Haynes' dream too far- fetched for their son Wesley.

On the other hand, Wesley, though he had the knack for legalese and was fascinated by legal issues, he saw himself as a musician and that's all. You say music and he is ready to *spit* you a tune. To him music was life! It had meaning. It was exhilarating!

He imagined playing music from sun up to sun down. With his pre-owned guitar recently acquired at a garage sale he roamed the town and villages in and around Mandeville emulating the likes of Jimmy Cliff, Bob Marley, Peter Tosh, The Beatles, The Temptations The Isley Brothers and many others; singing their songs and honing his musical craft. He was euphoric. On the other hand, his peers saw in him a musically possessed individual engulfed in a world of piped dreams.

As his "Adams apple" developed not only did his voice deepen more but his poignant rhythmic style was now becoming the talk of the town.

"That Wesley boy can sing you know," they said in *Patios.*

Now suddenly, the switch had flipped.

The neighbors, amongst themselves voiced *under their breath*, and in *Patois:*

"That Haynes' boy can really sing you know. Him has a very unique style."

Not only were the girls his age crushing hard on him, but older women alike. More so, not only was he like a magnet, he was beginning to mesmerize them with his musical style and pizzazz.

Megan and Sebastian were now finally buying into their son's talent as well as his determination. So much that they bought him his first electric guitar and an amplifier to go with it for his sixteenth birthday.

With these new musical toys Wesley played at neighborhood events *amped,* including the sweet potato fest. He wowed the crowd constantly with his music and converted many naysayers into believers.

CHAPTER 3

S uccess has a price to pay and not only was Wesley paying it by struggling financially as an artist, who bartended while pursuing his dream, but was simultaneously attracting friends and some enemies alike. Some people loved him but others without stipulation hated his guts.

Although many of those haters had seen and heard the most recent Garnet Silk in *Mamma Africa* and *Place In Your Heart*, Heavy D in *Mr. Big Stuff* and *Gyrlz,*

WHO SHOT THE SHERRIFF?

They Love Me, Sanchez in *Missing You* and *Never Diss De Man*, Buju Banton in *Murderer* and *Love Sponge* and Beres Hammond in *Tempted To Touch* and *Pull It Up*. They had cut their teeth on the musical vibes of Bob Marley and the Wailers in *I Shot The Sheriff* and *No Woman No Cry*, Peter Tosh in *Soon Come* and *Walk and Don't look Back*, Jimmy Cliff in *The Harder They Come* and *Many Rivers to Cross*, Dennis Brown in *Silhouette* and if *I Had The World*, Toots and The Maytals in *Sweet And Dandy*, Gregory Isaacs in *Night Nurse* and *My Number One*, and Third World in *Now That We Found Love* and *Sense of Purpose*.

They had danced to the poignant rhythm of American legends like Otis Redding in *Try A Little Tenderness* and *Hard To Handle*, Sam Cooke in *Cupid* and *Bring It On Home To Me*, The Temptations in *It Was Just My Imagination*, Jerry Butler in *For Your Precious Love* and *I Stand Accused*, the legendary Barry White in *Let the Music Play* and *You're The First, The Last, My Everything*, Al Green in *Love and Happiness* and *How Can You Mend A Broken Heart*, James Brown the Godfather of soul in *Sex Machine* and *Try Me*, Smokey Robinson in *You Really Got A Hold On Me* with the Miracles, and *Cruisin.'* Teddy Pendergrass in *T.K.O* and *Turn Off The Lights*. Plus, Marvin Gaye *in Sexual Healing* and *Lets Get It On*, and Michael Jackson in *Billie Jean* and *You Wanna Be Starting Something*.

Additionally, not forgetting: recently the soothing sounds of Luther Vandross in *Never Too Much* and *A*

House Is Not A Home, Jaheim in *Ghetto Love* and *Just In Case*, Brian McKnight in *Back At One* and *Crazy Love*, Lionel Ritchie in *Easy* and *Still*, and Babyface in *This Is for the Lover in You* and *Never Keeping Secrets*. As well as Usher in *Nice and Slow*. Plus the newcomer, Maxi Priest, on the reggae scene in his hit song *How Can We Ease The Pain?* and Shaggy in *It Wasn't Me*.

Nevertheless Wesley Haynes, a work in progress, what could he *spit* that was so exceptional? What can this *kid from the block* bring to the table? Many locals still queried despite his plodding emergence into the musical arena.

They couldn't comprehend. Not only that the visions in their minds were too nightmarish. But it was theirs and not Wesley's.

Those who hated Wesley did so mainly because they couldn't envision his dream of making it big and living out his true potential. So they laughed at and chipped away at his self-confidence. Even when they applauded, it was mediocre, on his behalf - full of envy and bigotry.

On many occasions those who thought less of Wesley would even attend neighborhood events where he performed in an effort to drag down the aspiring singer with their pessimism. Their hypocritical attitude was despicable to say the least. It got to Wesley Haynes on many occasions but he found in himself a way to rebound from their negativity.

WHO SHOT THE SHERRIFF?

Just like you can't hide the sound of thunder, the sight of lightning or the colors of a rainbow. So also, you cannot put a bushel on true talent mixed with persistence. Put it under a rock and it will roll that stone away. Even the police at the local station could not escape talking about Haynes as a potential rising music star and his upsurge was very, very noticeable.

John Brown, the descendant of a slave owner and the lead law enforcement officer in Mandeville wanted to stand out from the rest and dubbed himself *The Sherriff* – pronounced (*Sher-ef*). This veteran Sherriff who had struggled with alcoholism saw Haynes' success differently and filled with hatred looked for ways to nail Wesley Haynes at every opportunity. He had always nursed a big grudge for people with talent and now it was Wesley Haynes' turn. Why? Only Sherriff John Brown knew.

Sherriff Brown felt that any conviction brought against the young talent would sour the career of the rising star, who he called *Singer Man*. Brown would secretly but also jokingly ask his deputies:

"Anything yet on the *Singer Man*?"

When the response was in the vein of: 'nothing yet Sherriff.'

Brown would remark:

"If he sings he's got to have some flaws, he can't be that clean."

Brown knew deep in his psyche that one day he was going to spike Wesley Haynes to the *cross*, thereby, derailing his musical career. In his quest for sabotage, Sherriff Brown roamed the streets of Mandeville looking for any crime to which he could pin Haynes.

Although that Law Enforcement Department in Mandeville listed Brown's assignment on the board at the station indicating he was out looking for *Bad Boys* - a new term for law breakers. Brown would drive by the strip nightly where Haynes resided pretending he was doing a neighborhood watch to minimize criminal activity.

On multiple occasions Sherriff John Brown watched Haynes like a P.I. or some might say, like a hawk; by following him around the neighborhood oblivious to Haynes, in an unmarked police vehicle. On many weekends Brown would have his deputy join him in the stake outs so he could have ample time to follow Haynes around while the deputy concentrated on picking up other criminals. It was imperative they return to the station with a few citations at least.

Brown purposed in his mind: if Haynes' vehicle had a cracked windscreen, a malfunctioned wiper blade, a broken tail-light, a burnt out light bulb, a darker than normal tint, a going bald tire, a boisterous exhaust, expired registration, missing tags or anything he could manufacture or fabricate, be summed up as an infraction great or minor, he was going to cite Haynes and bring him in.

Brown had no problem being the *bad cop* that would prey over Wesley like a big hawk for any chance he could get to pounce. Brown was willing to bend the law, twist it or tweak it, or break it in order to come up with the catch inside his net – Wesley Haynes.

In his quest, made up of many late night stake outs, his searches were futile as Haynes always slipped through his grasp.

The singer knew the streets of Mandeville very well and oblivious to Browns' pursuit at this point used different routes to get home.

CHAPTER 4

O ne Friday night after performing at a club with his newly formed band of four, a bass guitarist Mike, a percussionist Max, a drummer Winston, and a female backup singer Britney, Wesley said one of his frequent long goodbyes and got inside his compact car heading home. The drive could normally take at least 20 minutes using alternate routes. On that particular night he took the familiar route which would get him home in 18 minutes. He realized that he was tired but found a way to stay wide eyed and bushy tailed.

The roads were clear at 2:00 AM except for a few returning home from the clubs motorists, and taxi cabs looking for the next fare, plus a few buyers and sellers working on their nocturnal high or their graveyard shift making money by peddling drugs.

Like the law of attraction Wesley *stepped on it* and soon he was accompanied by a trailing vehicle. Familiar with all the streets and intersections in Mandeville, Wesley thought about eluding the tailing vehicle and embarking on street race. So he took off through those well-known streets of Mandeville. Now with sirens and flashing red and blue lights the tailgater persisted. Haynes, sensing more than trouble pulled over to the side of the street.

Out of the Sheriff's car steps out Sherriff John Brown with numerous stripes on his lapel though most of them unjustly earned. He abruptly approaches Wesley's car posturing his rank and file status.

"What happen youth? You think this is a bloody Daytona Race Track? Speeding like a maniac! The speed limit signs are posted for a reason … too slow for offenders like you, huh?"

Says Sherriff Brown in *Patois*,

"Sir, it's been a long day and I was trying to get home soon. I really didn't mean to cause any harm. I am really a defensive …"

Sherriff Brown interrupts in *Patois*,

"Tell that to the Judge! You no see. I clocked you doing ninety in a forty mile an hour zone. That is fifty over the limit, a whole half a century. Plus you try to get away…"

"Sir I am not Brian Lara and wasn't playing cricket … I was just trying to get home."

Says Wesley,

"Oh you've got cricket jokes. Let me have a look at your driver's license, registration proof and insurance."

Demands Sherriff John Brown.

Haynes presents the Sherriff with the requested documents.

The Sherriff goes to his car and after reviewing Wesley Haynes' documents, instead of issuing him a traffic ticket, Sherriff Brown quickly returns to Wesley's car and remarks,

"Singer Man step out of the car."

No one had ever addressed Wesley using that name. Anyway, Haynes complies.

Sherriff Brown frisks him down for any possible weaponry. He is clean. The Sherriff roughs Wesley Haynes up and then cuffs him. He escorts him to his Sherriff car. There he shoves Haynes inside onto the back seat of his car. Haynes winces during the physical roughness.

"I am *The Sherriff*!" He reminded Haynes just in case he forgot who the brass cop in Mandeville was.

WHO SHOT THE SHERRIFF?

Sherriff Brown slams the door shut and returns to the singer's car. He rummages through the car. He finds Haynes' electric guitar, an amplifier and a notebook filled with written lyrics. He searches some more but finds nothing else he could use to incriminate the singer. With nothing else to attach Haynes to besides speeding, and possibly attempting to elude an officer, he drives him to the barracks where Haynes spends his first night behind bars after filling up a cup with his urine.

Haynes was permitted one phone call and that was made to his parents Megan and Sebastian. They were not at all happy that their son was spending the night in jail. Looking at the time on the clock showed that it was now 4:00 AM on that unforgettable Saturday. Later, that morning they readied themselves, made a trip to the police station to visit their son Wesley.

Driving to the station was uncomfortable for Megan and Sebastian Haynes. It was their first visit and they didn't know what to expect. They discussed the pros and the cons about Wesley's musical career choice. Did their son make the right decision to get all caught up in the musical industry? Was his dream too farfetched? If he had chosen a law profession maybe the law enforcers might be a bit more lenient with him regarding a traffic violation they reasoned.

Upon arriving at the police station Megan's and Sebastian's facial expressions clearly showed how much they abhorred the look and feel of the environment. Police officers were coming in and out fully loaded with sophisticated weapons as if they were returning from, or, going to war. Plus, calls were coming in regarding some of the most hideous crimes. They saw themselves in a very strange milieu as neither of his parents had ever visited a police station before.

Anyway, they posted bail and Wesley Haynes was released. His urine test came back negative for drug usage. As Brown had alleged that he had smelt marijuana odor in the car at the time when Wesley was pulled over. It was all a hoax; an attempt to nail the singer on drug charges. Even so, a charge was brought against Haynes for eluding a police officer in a high speed chase. That charge, though, was later dismissed.

CHAPTER 5

That one night spent in jail left a bad taste in Wesley's mouth. For the first time in his life he had been housed with criminals. These undesirables were made up of rapists, drug offenders, pimps, prostitutes, thieves, robbers, arsonists, and murderers; all awaiting arraignment. Most of whom, had no qualms confessing what they had done to wind up where they were.

The stats regarding the amount of black men who ended up going to jail or prison showed *they make up*

WHO SHOT THE SHERRIFF?

40.1% of the almost 2.1 million male inmates in the U.S and Jamaica. While almost 75% of them became second offenders. Additionally, *about 10.4% of the entire African-American male population in the United States aged 25 to 29 was incarcerated, by far the largest racial or ethnic group — by comparison, 2.4% of Hispanic men and 1.2% of white men in that same age group were incarcerated.* Compared to the stats in Jamaica those figures were very minuscule because of the densely Black populous.

Wesley examined those facts and felt they were despicable. His hometown of Mandeville in his eyes bore some resemblance and therefore wasn't very conducive to the growth of his potential. He felt like he was now a big fish swimming in a small pond filled with sharks alligators and crocodiles, which sought to devour him, namely one tough brass underhanded cop in Sherriff John Brown.

A few months later Wesley Haynes decided that he was going to take his skill east to Kingston the capital city. By now the rumor was out in Mandeville that Brown would do anything he could to put Haynes in the slammer. Haynes saw the handwriting on the wall and sought to change that condition.

Unfortunately for Sherriff Brown he felt like his ego was crushed when the charges brought against Wesley Haynes were dismissed.

Haynes had done his research and found that Kingston was accommodative to singers with skill and some, down to the core, sweat equity. Haynes was willing to pay that price by any means that were necessary. To Wesley Haynes the big city was a busy place where everyone was wrapped up in their own hustle and the flow, and he understood: genuine success was always up to the individual.

His parents Sebastian and Megan, when informed about his decision to move east weren't happy campers. Feeling like their only begotten was not making the right decision, they tried to get Wesley to change his mind. When asked: How he was going to survive? Wesley replied,

"I will find a day job and will be playing my music all night. While others are sleeping I will be hustling. *Bob Marley* spent a lot of time in Kingston."

He reminded his parents.

"Marley often returned to *Ocho Rios* where the air is cleaner and life is purer. Don't worry I will return when I make it big. I'm going to make it. I believe in the possibilities. This is my time."

Wesley reminded his parents.

"We still think that you need to give it some thought. Some real thought. Think it over son."

His mom encouraged.

Sebastian interjected,

"Son what you have gone through shouldn't give you reason to pack up and leave Mandeville. This is your birthplace."

"Dad it's all about the music. Music is the food of love. I've got to play it. I would rather soar with the eagles than scratch with these chickens."

Responds Wesley,

"Why don't you sleep on it? Think it over Wes."

His dad encouraged,

"Dad this is all about sticking to my mission. If I had taken up the legal profession and the opportunity arose for me to move to Kingston to work as an intern or paralegal at some unknown law firm. You would have said go get them Wesley. You were born to conquer. But because I've chosen my own brand of success – music, you are trying to persuade me to stay in Mandeville where the haters are many and the lovers are few. I would rather begin in a place where nobody knows me. Where my name has never been dragged through their court system, where no one destroys what I sow.

I love you both but I also love success because as a kid you always told me *I was born to succeed*. If I chose to be a janitor I would want to make sure that I became the best janitor there ever was: According, to the advice of the late Dr. Martin Luther King Jr."

Megan and Sebastian got the message. They realized their efforts were futile, in keeping Wesley in Mandeville, when he began to pack.

Wesley packed up his clothes in a suitcase that night. He placed his amplifier in a box, and his guitar in its case. His clothes he packed in another suitcase.

WHO SHOT THE SHERRIFF?

Early on the following morning he boarded a bus headed east to Kingston.

CHAPTER 6

Upon arriving in Kingston the big city, it didn't seem like all it was cut out to be. Most of the streets were filled with pot holes. The bus driver did Wesley a huge disfavor by driving first through the slum areas. One of the streets had an abandoned refrigerator in the middle of it. The bus took a detour in order to get to the next bus stop and away from the dumped household appliance.

Wesley very early was presented with a negative picture of his new city. He suddenly woke up to the realization that now he was in a city much different from Mandeville.

Wesley got off the bus close to Main Street. He needed a bite to eat having not packed a snack for the trip. He saw a restaurant close-by so he stopped in and purchased a beef patty and cocoa bread along with a cream soda. After devouring the meal he continued up towards Main Street.

Thomas, whom he met on the bus, saw him walking towards Main Street. Driving a little two-seater car Thomas pulled over, rolled the passenger window down and asked:

"Wesley, are you staying in this immediate area?" Wesley replied.

"I have not yet decided. I will figure it out."

"You are crazy mon. This is Kingston. Do you see what's going on all around you?"

Wesley looked half a block up Main Street and saw it not only occupied by gridlock vehicular traffic but pimps, prostitutes, Ministers of Parliament, drug dealers, vendors, card and domino players, robbers and people who if they could roll it, they smoked it. The *Weed* fumes saturated the mild, dense air. It seemed like suddenly *Ganja* smoking was legal. The partakers didn't smoke a little skinny joint but a big fat *newspaper rolled marijuana spiff*.

"Let me give you a lift to a safe place," said Thomas opening the passenger door. Wesley put his luggage on the back seat, and jumped in. The car took off through Main Street.

Thomas pulls up outside a small 25 room hotel. He told Wesley that he should check out the scene here until he's acclimated.

"You don't have to like it, it's not what you want, but it could be a means to help you get what you want, mon,"

Thomas said.

Thomas also informed Wesley that Clyde Gumbs the owner could use some help and suggested that Wesley introduce himself to Clyde and let him know that he is new in town and Thomas told him he might need some help with fetching groceries, cutting the grass, and emptying the trash in exchange for lodging, food and some pocket change.

Also, he gave Wesley his phone number and suggested Wesley call him to let him know how it worked out with Clyde.

Wesley took him up on it and moments later met with Clyde. The hotel owner Clyde stuttered and was tall and stocky built. He looked like a wrestler and in his mid-60s. Clyde interviewed Wesley. They bonded quickly. Clyde also a Mandeville native was very reassuring to Wesley the out-of-towner. He liked Wesley's ambitiousness and saw him fitting in nicely.

Clyde found extra chores for Wesley and paid him extra to do so. Wesley did not forget to call Thomas and thank him.

WHO SHOT THE SHERRIFF?

Soon Wesley was able to create some savings. So that when Clyde decided to put a for-sale sign on a van which was in the repair shop Wesley made him an offer. Clyde sold him the van for $500.00. Wesley continued working for Clyde in the day and at nights he rehearsed his music and wrote lyrics.

Everyone around Wesley smoked weed including Clyde who said his reason was medicinal. It wasn't long before Wesley Haynes indulged. Rehearsals were now like a *burning bush*. Like they say if you hang out with robbers at some point you would end up driving the getaway car and if you hang out with pigs you would find yourself rolling in the mud. Wesley was now rolling them up and getting his regular highs.

On the other hand, he stuck true to his objective, though sometimes as high as a kite while playing his music every night. Now Kingston, like most other Jamaican cities, was full of beautiful women. Even so, he didn't like what he saw in the women he met in Kingston as most just threw themselves at him. His heart was still set on his Britney in Mandeville. He longed for the day when he could see her again.

CHAPTER 7

Wesley Haynes' wages grew as he continued to save his money. He was earning a living but his heart was stuck back in Mandeville. One day he called Britney and asked if she would like to move to Kingston. Britney said yes without hesitation but was going to have to convince her parents that this move was going to pay off. Britney had her mind made up to elope but she ended up mentioning the move to her mom. Her mom

WHO SHOT THE SHERRIFF?

Christine and her dad James were not very happy that their only daughter was moving to Kingston. It was too far away from Mandeville. Plus, she was not about to have her nineteen year old daughter shack up with some singer; who all that he had going for himself in their eyes was raw potential, a guitar and an amplifier. Britney was raised in the church where she was immersed in biblical teachings, including that sex came after marriage. Her mom also believed in those related concepts.

Even so, after several days of pleading with her mom to release the reigns, her mom finally consented that she go under one condition: She was not going to get pregnant before marriage like her mom Christine did. Britney gave her mom her word and the following day she headed east on a bus bound for the capital city of Kingston.

Wesley rented and moved into an apartment on 'Main Street.' Britney arrived from Mandeville a few days later. She was so excited to see him again. It wasn't long after the reunion though, someone stole Wesley's van. Now they were without transportation. Not only did they need it to get around in Kingston but the van was needed by Wesley in order to continue fetching groceries for his boss Clyde Gumbs. So like sliding downhill, Wesley was rendered not only unemployed but, no groceries came from Clyde as a result of his no show-up.

WHO SHOT THE SHERRIFF?

For a few weeks they ate corn meal porridge, peanut butter and jelly sandwiches, washing the meal down with *sweet water*. While Wesley was without transportation, he one day got on the bus and visited the neighborhood bank to acquire a loan. He was met and interviewed by Mrs. Jacobs the loan officer. She welcomed him and served him some Jamaican Blue Mountain Coffee.

As they sat down to discuss his banking needs. Wesley requested a loan of $10,000.00. Getting back on his feet was a priority and that amount could go a long way. Mrs. Jacobs ran his credit report. From the look on her face it didn't look satisfactory. Then she broke the news letting Wesley know she had to deny him credit. Wesley returned home for yet another day of cornmeal porridge, peanut and jelly sandwiches, and *sweet water*.

Later that night the Kingston Police called and notified Wesley they had found his vehicle. He made arrangements to pick it up the following morning. When he recovered the van it was not only out of alignment it was decorated on one side with graffiti. His dream tank was suddenly convoluted with nightmares and this domino effect was like a parasite eating away at him.

Throughout this entire ordeal, Wesley was smart enough to keep in touch with Clyde.

In an effort to downsize Clyde decided to sell the hotel and to move to a senior citizen home across town. Clyde knew the owners of most of the restaurants and clubs in Kingston including Milton Rogers who owned *Michael's Bar and Grill*. Clyde's entrepreneur buddies had it going on in the big city. So Clyde made some phone calls on Wesley's behalf. *Michael's Bar and Grill* invited Haynes in for his debut performance.

Haynes bought Britney a nice sexy dress for the event. She liked it and dressed to the nines for the occasion. Britney did backup vocals while Wesley did vocals and played his guitar. They *spat* some familiar *covers*. Clyde and Thomas also attended the event. They had a blast and experienced firsthand, Wesley, the man behind his music.

Michael's brought in Wesley and Britney to perform on Thursday and Friday nights every week. The patrons enjoyed their music. As the word spread about their musical style, their weekly calendar all of a sudden was fully booked. After most sessions which wrapped at 2:00 AM Wesley and Britney would go to their crib on Main Street and stay awake counting up twenty, ten, five and one dollar bills. They were booking gig after gig and they liked the flow.

Two weeks later they were joined by the other members of the band. Wesley drove the van to their gigs. He dropped his band members off at their *yard* after their musical performances each night.

In addition to using *covers* of other singers like Bob Marley, Jimmy Cliff, Steele Pulse, Lionel Richie, Peter

Tosh, Dennis Brown, James Brown and the like, they developed the habit of *spitting* their own tracks. They wrote and practiced extensively for hours. Someone always brought in the weed to their sessions as they took turns. That habit was now evolving in their little clique.

One night after playing at a club and packing up their equipment, Wesley was approached by a man and his wife. The man, a Jamaican national who later revealed his identity as Bill Parsons, and a Mandeville extract: He told Haynes that he was looking for young fresh talent to go into the studio and record. Bottom line he was in the new talent discovery business. And that Haynes should give him a call to further discuss the possibilities. Parsons had heard about Haynes from his long-time friend Milton Rogers.

Haynes' band members overheard the conversation and the night trip to their homes took on a different tone. They were laughing and cutting up while reminiscing about their tenure in Mandeville. They felt that coming east was about to pay off big dividends.

Max the percussionist had to break up with his girlfriend Sofia in order to move to Kingstown. In a heated quarrel regarding the move she told him that it's either Kingston or her. He chose Kingston.

Mike the bass guitarist had no strings attached. If the band members said they were going to the moon, he was all in. In his eyes Wesley and Britney were like the characters *Henny Penny* and *Ducky Lucky* and he was willing to follow.

Winston, on the other hand decided to give up his part time job as a fitness trainer. A job he had held for many years. It was tough breaking ties, not knowing when he was going to be able to pay his bills and continue saving ten percent of his income as he was accustomed to.

But now it seemed like things were getting ready to turn around for the better.

"Most people seek out these kinds of opportunities but this one sought us out."

Said Haynes, under his smile enthused breath.

Getting home that night, in their present happy mindset, felt like one escalated elevated ride. Britney was ecstatic. She saw herself being able to shop *till she dropped* and wear the kind of attire real performers are able to.

Wesley Haynes called Bill Parsons the following day and set up a time to meet. This feel good attitude was now so contagious it transpired into every note they played and every lyric they *spat*. Their performances now took on true meaning as they sang with passion and purpose and with vision as well.

Those nights and days leading up to the interview seemed shortened as the anticipated day to the meeting drew closer - to be followed by possible studio time.

CHAPTER 8

The day of the meeting soon arrived and Wesley Haynes showed up at Bill Parson's office. Haynes wanting the deck stacked on his side dressed in neat and clean upscale casuals. He couldn't afford a car wash for the van which had recently been stolen and graphitized, so he parked it a little distance away from the building so as not to feel embarrassed and above all outclassed by the Mercedes Benzes and Cadillac SUV's he expected to find parked outside Bill's office. Haynes was right as he parked the van around the corner and walked to the office he discovered a parking lot filled with some of the most desirable automobiles in the world. Bill Parson's parking spot from Wesley's point of view had his name on it: RESERVED FOR BILL PARSONS. Wesley Haynes quickly pressed the buzzer to the door and announced himself. A woman answered. As he entered through the revolving glass door of this middle-sized office he realized that the woman with Bill that night at the club also worked there at the studio. Dressed in a beautiful red dress the woman addressed:

"I am Rose Best–Parsons, Bill is expecting you. He is with another client and should be out shortly."

Rose assured.

It wasn't long after taking a seat that Wesley was escorted by Rose to Bill's office with a signed contract and a smile on her face. In the interim, the other client, a woman in her early twenties made her exit from Bill's office. Bill extended his hand and shook Haynes'. The two men talked about vision and potential for a while after breaking more of the ice.

Later Bill Parsons took Wesley on a tour of the back studio lot. Bill talked with Wesley about the possibilities of taking his music all the way to the top. After the tour of the studio they returned to the office. This was new for Wesley; no one had ever taken him by the hand in his musical career. Haynes felt like he had found his mentor in Bill Parsons.

As a result of that meeting, Haynes and his band booked their first recording session and were scheduled for three weeks from that date. Wesley left the office elated as he was clearly seeing his dream materialize. In his mind coming east was paying off big time.

Haynes couldn't wait to break the great news to the members of the band and did. They, waiting for his return at a local restaurant were beside themselves upon learning that they were booked for a studio recording session and that Bill Parsons was interested in signing them. Additionally realizing they had three more weeks to get themselves ready before the recording. Their rehearsals took on major significance and their gigs were events which made bodies of their audience tingle.

They were evolving as a superb talented group. They had a sense of purpose. Max, the percussionist after one Friday night gig said that Wesley not only sang like a man possessed but he heard his guitar speak on separate occasions.

THAT DAY CAME and they entered the studio ready to lay down their tracks. Upon arriving at the studio they were met by "Big Bubba" the engineer, an Afro-Asian man in his mid-forties. Big Bubba did his pre-recording spiel. Moments later, they were set up to record their first song, and did they give it all they got. At the end of the session, when the recording studio door opened, they stepped out electrified. Their song *This Is My Time* was indeed the way they were feeling and they wanted the rest of the world to know.

Bill Parsons was not present at the studio session but he walked in as soon as Big Bubba was getting ready to do a playback for Wesley and his band members. Parsons was mesmerized after Bubba his engineer pressed playback. So were the members of the entire band. Wesley asked for a rough copy, and Bill Parsons burned him a copy of the recording pending a scheduled mixing session.

Wesley Haynes and his posse left the studio on an all-time high and returned to their dwellings more stoked than when they first came together or even when first made their move to Kingston. Was it hard for them to sleep that night? You bet! It was. They stayed awake thinking about the possibilities along the way.

However, like those twisted ironies of life which none of us understand that night, tragedy struck hard. Unfortunately, for Bill Parsons he did not make it home that night. While leaving the studio's parking lot he was approached by two armed gunmen who not only robbed him by taking his wallet and the keys to his Mercedes Benz. They pumped several bullets into his body, leaving him for dead. As if that wasn't enough they broke into the recording studio and walked off with studio equipment along with the mixer and microphones.

The following morning as the local Television stations reported the news, Wesley held Britney in his arms, in tears. The man who was opening the door to their career now no longer existed. Big Bubba, it was alleged had already made it home when the incident occurred. Bubba stated as was reported to Wesley by Rose:

"Bill stayed at the studio after Big Bubba left and was listening to that song over and over again. They both felt they had a great song and couldn't wait to have it mixed and distributed."

The tragedy hit home to the band members in many ways. Was this foul play? Their newly recorded song was left inside the archives of the stolen mixing equipment. But more so their newly acquired mentor and major music connection had lost his life. It was tough for the band members to come to grips with the whole situation.

CHAPTER 9

L ater that evening before the band's regular practice session, the five band members Max, Mike, Winston, Britney and Wesley stopped at the neighborhood pharmacy where they bought a sympathy card. Before rehearsing they all signed the card and sent it to Rose Best–Parsons along with a bouquet of flowers. For several weeks later they not only mourned the loss of Bill Parsons but also the loss of the master recording of their first song.

On the other hand, Wesley Haynes was happy he requested a copy of the song so he could take home with him. Even though he wasn't optimistic about it being of superb quality, he felt like there was some value in the copy and wanted to listen to it that night after the session.

In the meantime, Britney felt like all they had come to Kingston to accomplish was falling apart. She and Wesley argued and she indicated she wanted to return to Mandeville. As a matter of fact she took it one step further and began packing up her things. One of the things she said was:

"My mom told me not to move to Kingston with a man who all he had going for him was some potential, a guitar and an amplifier but I did."

Wesley was torn by those words. He loved Britney madly. Trying the best he could do to convince her to stay seemed not to be working out. He told her things would get better. Even so, to her, the road to success was getting harder and her patience was growing thin. Looking across at the two suitcases she left the apartment in an effort to clear her head.

Without his knowledge, his girl Britney went to the park to jog and do her afternoon meditating to finalize her move back to Mandeville. While at the park she ran into a woman who worked as a secretary at a recording studio in Kingston. They talked briefly.

Wesley stayed on the phone while Britney was out the house and made a series of phone calls in an effort to find someone who would take on his unfinished project, either re-record a session or mix the tracks which he held on to. He got hit with rejection after rejection. It was now mid-afternoon after making phone calls to no avail. Wesley, right when he was about to push the project aside he heard Britney walk in through the kitchen.

"Don't give up! I met someone who could probably help us mix and duplicate that song." She remarked.

"Really?"

Asks Wesley,

"Yes I do. I don't know how much they will charge us but as a secretary she might be able to draw us some favors."

Replies Britney,

"How come you did not mention that before now? You are holding out on a brother aren't you?"

Responds Wesley,

"I just met her at the park, Wesley."

Britney responds,

Britney grabs the phone, dials and strokes Wesley's head while she waits through the dial tone. The phone rings for a while. No one picks up. She redials and finally, Grace the secretary picks up.

"Hey Grace, its Britney! We met at the park earlier today. I realize you are just back from lunch..."

"Yes, we did and how are you? I like your hairstyle, I'll see if my hairdresser can hook me up with such a hairdo. Girl, I have to come and check out one of your gigs around town. When and where are you playing next?"

Asks Grace.

Britney is now animated.

"We'll be at *Michael's Bar and Grill* this Thursday and Friday evening. Drop by so we can hang a bit and plus you'll get to meet Wesley and the rest of the band members… I've been telling you about."

Says Britney,

"Sure thing I can do Friday night. I will get a babysitter. I'll see you there. Got to go; my phone is ringing off the hook. Plus the big boss is making his presence felt."

Grace says to Britney as she abruptly aborts the phone conversation.

"She'll be at *Michael's* on Friday night, Wesley."

Says Britney as she joins Wesley on the couch. Now they are both staring at the two packed suitcases in the living room and the money for the one way bus ticket on the center table.

"Can she or can't she help solve the problem?"

Asks Wesley.

"I haven't asked her as yet. First she'll have to meet you and the band. Then we'll girl talk a little. Then I will do my BTW. Women believe in the four-play process but guys want it right away."

Responds Britney.

"Is that our next song?"

Says Wesley as he kisses her on the lips.

WHO SHOT THE SHERRIFF?

The phone rings. Wesley grabs it on the second ring. Any news at this point is great news. Not only to move the project along he visualizes, but also, for keeping the love of his life Britney there in Kingston.

It's Big Bubba, the engineer.

Bubba informs Wesley that a reliable source just informed him that the Mandeville Sheriff's Department were connected to the robbery and shooting death of Bill Parsons. Big Bubba stated that Parsons had owned several acres of marijuana plantations in the hills of Manchester, north of Mandeville. Also that it wasn't a robbery; it was a cold hit - and organized sting which brought down the entrepreneur and record producer Bill Parsons.

Wesley asks Bubba,

"Is there anything you can do to help us move the project along?

"There is nothing you can do with that song in your hand. If it's mixed it will be full of scratches and right now I have no connections to set you up with for a new recording session. So for the moment you may just have to can it!"

Britney, still sitting on the couch and staring at Wesley, dumbfounded and discombobulated about Bill's death realizes the plot was not the news she wanted to hear. Not the way to say goodbye to the man who in such a short time opened the door to their musical career.

She regains her presence of mind and asks,

WHO SHOT THE SHERRIFF?

"What's up Wes? Is it what I'm hearing? Sherriff John Brown? He struck again, that hatemonger?"
"Sherriff again!
Says Wesley,
Britney's jaw drops as it finally begins sinking in that what she is hearing is for real.
Wesley continues,
"Apparently they were responsible for the death of Mr. Bill Parsons. I don't get it. If they work as cops in the city of Mandeville.... Why are they carrying out raids in Kingston? That's totally outside of their jurisdiction."

LATER THAT DAY SEVERAL HELICOPTERS surveyed marijuana plantations in Manchester. In the interim, Jamaican Police moved in, accompanied by U.S army personnel. They torched many *Ganja* plantations burning down marijuana trees and plantation houses. Ten Jamaican nationals were shot and killed during the confrontation with the police infantry and army personnel.

It was believed that the men killed were responsible for plantation operations and worked for the now deceased Bill Parsons.

Additionally, it was also reported that some areas of the more than half-mile-square (kilometer-square) marijuana plantation resembled a nursery, with small plants in different stages of growth. Other parts were like mature corn fields with neat rows of forest green plants rising more than six feet to a protective mesh shielding the expanse of plants.

From the aerial view, via helicopters it was said that it looked like a giant square of asphalt secluded in the Valley areas of Manchester.

Minutes after the plantations went up in smoke, dark black gray ash clouds hovered over Mandeville covering it like a thick dark blanket.

Many locals watching the inferno wished they had the opportunity to fetch a few hundred pounds of that weed prior to it going up in smoke. With its fantastic market value most of them would have been set for life.

As a result of the burning weed, the *contact* from those smoke laden clouds was distributed and felt in many low lying areas of the city of Mandeville. Many residents of Mandeville, it was reported who never partook of the substance not even medicinally, received their first Ganga high for free - and unchallenged by the law.

CHAPTER 10

It was Friday night at *Michael's Bar and Grill* in Kingston. The DJ was spinning vinyl while the band members set up their equipment on stage. A few patrons were mingling; enjoying cocktails and appetizers, while others got their groove on *dubbing it* out on the dance floor. All roads seemed to lead under the strobe lights. Grace showed up as promised. She was dressed to the nines. Britney on stage, setting up the microphone stands, spotted her as soon as she entered the room. Britney met with her moments later and then introduced her to Wesley and other members of the band. Grace had a few glasses of Merlot while she *chit chatted* with Britney elated by her make-over hairstyle.

Suddenly the DJ announced the band's upcoming on-stage appearance scheduled to occur in the next three minutes. As a result of that 3 minute warning, many rushed to the bar to get a drink before the band played.

The band took the stage and opened up with *Thank you Lord* then segued into *THIS IS MY TIME*. The audience were now sucked into the musical interlude and were on their feet dancing and cheering. Amongst them was Grace, *partying hearty* - applauding while she danced.

During the intermission Grace talked again with Wesley. She stated how much she liked the song and was happy to have met Britney and able to attend the night's event. Wesley then thanked her for coming and arranged to drop off a copy of the song the next morning.

Grace's boss Alston Beckles liked the song and decided to host a recording session. Wesley showed up with his band a few days later to the studio and the song was in the can and made ready for distribution a few weeks later.

Haynes and his band members were invited to the studio to hear a preview. They liked it. So did the studio. Grace got on the phone immediately pitching the song. At the end of that same afternoon she had placed calls to several radio stations not only in Jamaica but in the U.S. Holland and the United Kingdom as well. Most of them bought into the hype and decided to preview the song during that same week. Some radio station producers couldn't wait to get their hands on a copy.

Leaving the studio on cloud nine, the band members boarded their van, put in the CD and rocked the song as they partied on their way home.

THAT NIGHT they thought about taking off but showed up at their night gig instead. Before the first intermission they sang their new release and handed out a few copies. Even the DJ rocked the song while their band took an intermission.

After the break with the crowd yelling "*This Is My Time,*" the band opened up with *This Is My Time*. The audience loved the song and wanted more but their appetite was only wetted with a diminutive reprise version.

The following week Haynes' song lit up the airwaves in Jamaica and around the world. In less than three weeks it climbed to Number One on the music charts.

Things began to change with the air of success. The band now booked bigger and better gigs and, even upgraded their musical equipments. Every exclusive nightclub in Kingston wanted them. All of their performances were now not only sold out events but unforgettable performances.

Countries overseas including China, Japan, Holland, Germany, Australia, the United Kingdom, Brazil, the U.S, and hosts of other nations were jamming the song not only on radio but at clubs and most music related events. Concert venues throughout the U.S. also joined the list of callers requesting a musical performance.

With the well-deserved success, the band members upgraded their lifestyles. Instead of using the one van as a means of transportation, they each were able to afford their own vehicle. Britney went on a much needed shopping spree.

As the sales of the record soared Grace continued to drive momentum using referral after referral to push its sales.

The song held the Number One spot on the charts for over twelve weeks. It was obvious that Mandeville's rising star had risen though in a different town than his hometown. Coming east had brought success to Wesley Haynes.

The singer wisely put some money into savings. Not only did he upgrade to a white fully loaded *drop top*, it was now just one in his fleet of many automobiles. Money flowed in like money was going out of style.

On a beautiful sunny day Wesley decided to drive his *drop top* to his neighborhood bank where he still did his banking. He wondered how Mrs. Jacobs was doing. In his mind a convertible car and a *drive-thru* went well together. So he chose the drive-thru versus going inside the bank that day. As he pulled up into the driveway there was Mrs. Jacobs at the drive-thru window.

Wesley handed her the deposit slip. She read it, as stated, a $10,000.00 deposit. He opened his bag which was sitting on the rear seat and handed her stacks of one dollar bills. The money counting machine at the bank was inoperative on that sunny Friday afternoon. So Mrs. Jacobs had to count the bills manually. Before proceeding she told Wesley the machine mal-functioned so to bear with her as she counted the bills by hand.

Wesley told her with a smile:

"That's okay. I don't have anywhere to go. I am not in any hurry. I will wait until you are finished."

While she counted the bills, Wesley played songs like: *This Is My Time*, *The Harder They Come*, *I Am Gonna Use What I Got,* and *Black Man Redemption* along with others from his MP3 collection.

While the 10, 000 one dollar bills were being counted by Mrs. Jacobs, the motorists in tow of Wesley began tooting their horns in desperation. The counting took a while and aggravated the heck out of them. Suddenly there was a mini traffic-jam at the bank's parking lot as cars were seen reversing out of the drive-thru. Those drivers later opted to go inside the bank and carry out their transactions in a peeved manner.

Wesley, after that stunned look on Mrs. Jacobs' face collected his deposit slip, folded it neatly, put it inside his wallet and drove off and out of the bank's drive-thru.

CHAPTER 11

It was during the era when the U.S placed an embargo on the Caribbean banana trade. They demanded fair trade at The Lomé Convention in September 1997. Caribbean bananas are normally grown on small, family-run farms and were about to take a hit. A September 1997 World Trade Organization (WTO) decision pressured by the US, backed by companies like *Chiquita*, had meant that these local producers were forced to compete on a "level playing field" with giant multinationals and Latin-American "dollar" bananas. Entering into this pact with South America in more ways than one benefitted *Chiquita* who apparently was near bankruptcy.

It was a tough one for farmers in the islands. Owing to this restriction, most farmers who harvested bananas resorted to growing marijuana as a substitute crop. It became known to the U.S government and in collaboration with the local government they sent in helicopters and members of their armed forces to torch the *Ganja* crops.

In the interim, Colombia kept growing their marijuana produce in abundance. So much so, that, they were able to supply the glut in the marketplace. If you bought some weed in the Caribbean during the burning of the plantations raids, rest assured it was Colombian. It wasn't long before the U.S backed off from the torching of crops. The hillsides of Manchester and other torched plantations in Jamaica soon became green again.

It was believed that the ash from those fires served as fertilizer to grow the now luscious Ganja trees. Profits soared in the marijuana market.

Not only did *Kingstonians* now get most of their weed from the hillsides of Mandeville but it served as a constant supplier for Canada and the U. S and the U.K. as well.

Jamaican police along with American military infantry using helicopters once again embarked into the hills of Mandeville in an attempt to destroy their Ganja crops. Unfortunately they met with strong resistance from the locals who not only slowed their entrance into the hills but in some cases blocked the streets with used furniture and other major appliances, trapping and killing the "pigs" – another name for the police. *Ganja* farmers fired many rounds off at will, injuring and killing some of these anti-drugs supporters.

Profits now soared from the Mandeville plantations. The *Ganja* boom attracted investors including Wesley Haynes and others who acquired several acres of land back in Haynes' hometown.

The word leaked to Sherriff John Brown not only that Haynes had struck it big with his music but that he was cashing in on the profits from the booming narcotics industry in Jamaica. So he sent his Deputy Ron Charles to Kingston to capture Haynes and bring him back to Mandeville for interrogation.

By this time Wesley Haynes had already acquired several bodyguards to keep a lot of people at bay. His celebrity status was emerging rapidly whether he wanted to or not. Whenever and wherever he performed it was a known fact that the singer's heavily guarded entourage was present.

Meanwhile, Wesley Haynes returned to Mandeville for the first time since he moved to Kingston. He spent only the weekend and assisted in the move of his parents Megan and Sebastian out of Jamaica to a new home in Miami, Florida. This gift was a total surprise to the now retired couple. Never wanting to leave Mandeville, they weren't sure how they were going to fit in. But they adjusted and became acclimated swiftly despite their retirement status.

Sheriff John Brown's deputy oblivious of security surrounding Wesley Haynes along with his weekend trip to Mandeville went into Kingston in search of Wesley Haynes solo. Not only did he not find Haynes but found nothing in the drug trafficking business to attach Haynes to. People in Kingston were tight lipped about Wesley Haynes' affairs.

During that unofficial hunt for Haynes Deputy Ron Charles traveled from night club to night club and restaurant to restaurant. Yet he did not find Wesley Haynes.

IN THE INTERIM, Wesley and Britney along with their parents and band members were now in Miami. The two singers after going back and forth with the timeframe and a locale finally decided to tie the knot and have a private wedding in Miami before heading to Paris for their honeymoon.

So the Sheriff's deputy returned to Mandeville *empty handed*. This did not sit well with his boss Sheriff John Brown who questioned his deputy's incompetence for failing to deliver Wesley Haynes.

WHO SHOT THE SHERRIFF?

Brown later stated to another Deputy, that Deputy Charles was not on the same page bringing in Wesley Haynes, and felt that Haynes was paying the Deputy off in order to *cool it.*

Brown wanted Haynes and would not settle for less than just that. This was now his burning desire, it was his ultimate obsession. The Sherriff vowed that he would catch Haynes and bring him to justice in his hometown of Mandeville someday.

CHAPTER 12

When the Deputy Ron Charles returned to Mandeville without Wesley Haynes in the net, Sherriff John Brown later decided that he would pick up the *rod* and go after the Singer Man himself. He toyed with the idea of driving to Montego Bay and flying out to Kingston. But Brown wanted to do things somewhat incognito despite his objective. He was concerned about masking the suspicion that he was really after Haynes, in case it all blew up in his face.

The word had been out that he had a vendetta against Wesley Haynes in Mandeville, though not yet in most other cities. But, every trap he set Haynes seemed to be breaking out of that net. This displeased the Sherriff very much.

So, Brown left for Kingston accompanied by five other Deputy Officers in a large van. Ron Charles was not with them on the trip; Brown wanted him to stay put for allegedly *cooling it*. They made the van their final choice of transportation because it was roomy, brand new and fully loaded. Plus news came in that Haynes had acquired an elite armed entourage so they had to be prepared against possible retaliation by the Haynes' posse.

In that event, they needed to load up on as much weaponry as possible onto the van. Several AK45s were amongst their very eclectic handpicked arsenal.

Upon arriving in Kingston, Brown found it necessary to use a separate vehicle. So he rented an unmarked sedan luxury car and went undercover through the streets of Kingston. Prior to their daily manhunt which was carried out mostly at nights when the clubs were in operation they came together to debrief.

One night Brown and his team went looking for Haynes at *Michael's*. He had received a tip from the Kingston Sheriff Department that Haynes performed there on Thursday and Friday nights. Sherriff Brown showed up like a hungry lion and made his way inside the club - solo. While his van and crew staked out a few blocks away waiting to be dispatched if necessary.

Upon entering the club he came up against the owner, Milton Rogers. Rogers knew about Sherriff John Brown's vendetta against Haynes. So he told him Haynes was not there and that he should let the Police in Kingston handle the business in Kingston.

Sherriff John Brown didn't like anyone talking to him in that manner. After all he was THE SHERRIFF.

On the other hand, Rogers was a tough cookie and wasn't into bowing down to any Kingston cop much less an out of town law enforcement officer. Plus, it was talked about by some of Roger's local law enforcement contacts, regarding how much money Sherriff Brown's office was spending to try and bring down Wesley Haynes.

Rogers had even questioned as to why that money wasn't being used to build schools and provide a better system of education for the local residents in Mandeville. Rogers knew that Mandeville had Sheriff John Brown's back for far too long. That's why Brown got away with whatever he chose to do. Both men argued for a while resulting in Brown displaying his gun during the scorching verbal exchange. Rogers though was not at all intimidated. Sherriff Brown later walked out of the club challenged.

WHO SHOT THE SHERRIFF?

Although his objective in visiting Kingston was to bring in Haynes, he had to find a way to get back at Rogers for his trash talking. So to prove his authority he visited *The Crow's Nest,* a chic nightclub owned by Rogers overlooking Kingston. Some notables who frequented this joint included the late Bill Parsons. This served as a hole in the wall for most entertainers in the capital city.

Brown pulled up outside in his unmarked vehicle, surveyed the premises and then called in his team to make arrests. Outside the *Crow's Nest,* they arrested more than two dozen men and women made up mostly of patrons who had had records as pimps, prostitutes and drug dealers. Officers jumped out of the van like S.W.A.T in action, displaying their sophisticated arsenal of weaponry. Sherriff Brown was about to capture some *bad boys* and on Milton Roger's premises.

In his mind he didn't get what he wanted so he took what he could get. Later not only did the Kingston Police take those individuals to jail, but Brown was able to help orchestrate putting a chain and lock on *The Crow's Nest* claiming it was a drug depot. Brown was able to that because of his major connections in law enforcement throughout Jamaica, and that's just the way it flowed. Even so, the man he mostly wanted was still at large in his eyes and on the hustle.

WHO SHOT THE SHERRIFF?

They continued searching in that city for Haynes, and at other places they thought the singer would frequent, their search turned up futile.

On the streets the word from pessimistic vagrants and the mentally insane voiced that Haynes was hiding in a bunker back in Mandeville.

Sherriff John Brown did not buy into the epiphany of the bunker philosophy. He was cognizant of the fact that if one was there in Mandeville, he would have been the first to know about it. He was the *Sherriff* and he had it like that.

Those intellectuals on the other hand, knew better. They knew that Haynes was not a fugitive and he was well protected against the vindictive Sherriff John Brown. After all the word was out and debated amongst them that "The Sherriff was after Wesley Haynes."

It was later learned as news soon circulated that Wesley Haynes and Britney had gotten married in the U.S. and after honeymooning were embarking on an impromptu tour. This tour was centered on the east coast from Tampa, Florida to Boston, Massachusetts. Sherriff Brown was sadly disappointed when he got the news as he was set on bringing home - that big fish to be fried and sautéed – Wesley Haynes.

Overseas, Americans were not only talking about the singer's music in Barber Shops, Hair Salons, Coffee Shops, Eateries, Subway Stations, Airports and Bus Stations; they were bopping to the beat of his music on office elevators and during smoke breaks, even prisoners were in the mix at their yard.

Whenever people wanting to be fit worked out at the local gyms or jog down the street they were playing his music from Central Park in New York City to Disneyworld in Florida and Disneyland in California.

Frustratingly and in disgust, Sherriff John Brown returned back to Mandeville just like his deputy did – empty handed. Except that he arrested some *bad boys* and thought about every possible horrible thing he would do to Haynes when he would be captured.

CHAPTER 13

For several weeks Sherriff John Brown shuffled papers filled with erroneous information presented to him: stating Haynes had finished his U.S. tour and returned to roost in Mandeville. So once again he continued his frequent stake outs.

Retrospectively, the American concert venues proved differently for Haynes; he and his band were still appearing at scheduled events throughout the U.S, while Brown continued to relentlessly and mistakenly track him down in Jamaica.

One day while going through his paper shuffling routine a wire came across his desk that a ship loaded with marijuana was found adrift off the coast of Port Antonio. It was believed according to reporters that Haynes had ties to this vessel as it was registered to a U.S. Miami address once used by the singer.

Although it was too early to pinpoint Haynes' direct involvement as information remained sketchy. Sherriff John Brown felt optimistic that Haynes was connected in one way or the other. And if Haynes was connected this was Brown's chance to have the singer put away for good in Jamaican prison where even the stray dogs get treated better; as the word on the street described those prison conditions. So Sherriff John Brown took a leave of absence from the Mandeville office in order to visit Port Antonio in an attempt to carry out his private independent investigation on the origin of the narcotics and ship's owner.

It was not an easy task for him to get involved in the investigation as he had planned. The Port Antonio Police Department wanted full access to that boat load of weed. They wanted no out of Towner's next to it, not even some of their own policemen.

Port Antonio was said to have strong ties to some of the most powerful drug cartels. Plus, the corrupt police department in that city had an affinity with the Colombian Drug Cartels; they brought in revenue unmatched by any other Caribbean city from San Juan in Puerto Rico to Port of Spain in Trinidad and Georgetown, Guyana.

Luckily for Sherriff Brown one of his colleagues Lieutenant Samuel Graves worked at the Port Antonio Police Department and had some seniority which he exercised in bringing Sherriff Brown on board the investigative team made up of top brass narcotics agents from Port Antonio. Brown though had to get accustomed to less seniority but he adjusted his status in order to join the investigative team.

Samuel Graves on the other hand, claimed that Brown was his part-time understudy. So they went to work unraveling the case pertaining to the ship.

Sherriff John Brown was right this time around as singer Wesley Haynes, it was alleged co-owned the ship that went adrift with over 100 bags of weed. Each crocus bag contained at least fifty pounds of chronic weed bound for Miami. The stench was overwhelming coming from that loaded anchored ship.

Prior to the ship going adrift, Brown had also been aggressively investigating the shipping of marijuana from Jamaica. He was led to believe whoever handled the trade had a great degree of sophistication because no arrests were made on the transportation end of the trade. Haynes was allegedly in the mix and if this could be validated, Sherriff Brown was coming after him.

BEFORE LEAVING FOR PORT ANTONIO, the Sherriff had a few rounds of liquor in order to celebrate in advance what in his eyes way going to be his greatest accomplishment ever since his hate parade against the singer began.

During the week long full-fledged investigation it was determined the singer was involved.

As a result of his findings, Jamaican authorities requested that Haynes be brought back to Jamaica in order to stand trial.

Haynes' Madison Square Garden performance had to be cancelled and Haynes returned to his hometown Mandeville in handcuffs to be arraigned before the prominent Judge Christopher Bailey.

CHAPTER 14

During the trial which lasted for almost 6 months, attorneys for Haynes did all they could to remind jurors that Wesley Haynes was an emerging international reggae star, whose music was making an impact on the lives of many.

Additionally, during the tenure of the hearing, numerous photos of Wesley Haynes were distributed as flyers outside the Mandeville courthouse.

On the other hand, his hit single CD was selling like hot cakes in many places; the U.S., Europe, France, Holland, Asia, The United Kingdom, Germany, and Jamaican cities, more so in Mandeville.

After six months of hearings in the Mandeville court-house, the Mandeville and recently Miami resident, 27 year old Wesley Haynes who had faced 10 years to life in prison was sentenced after un-swayed jurors found him guilty of drug trafficking.

Sherriff John Brown testified against Haynes at the hearing. He stated: When he arrested Haynes for a speeding late one Friday night, the car in which Haynes committed the offense smelled like Ganja. He claimed that the singer took off on a high speed chase through the streets of Mandeville. He further testified that he did not charge the singer for smoking the substance; because the substance nor any other material portion of its residue was found in the car, during the search which he orchestrated while Haynes was in handcuffs.

Sherriff John Brown made sure he cleverly sounded like he had given *those breaks* to Haynes during his testimony at the hearing. He did not want to be portrayed as if he had a vendetta against the singer. Jimmy Cliff *spat* a song called *Hypocrites* and this was the Sherriff's MO – being hypocritical. He had to keep that façade on the down low based on who he was dealing with and the prevailing mitigating set of circumstances.

Additionally, Brown said that a urine test carried out on the singer proved negative for narcotics. But that the singer was speeding like someone who was apparently high on something.

Judge Christopher Bailey also a high-flying resident of Mandeville showed no bias and sentenced Wesley Haynes to 10 years in prison for narcotics trafficking. Dozens of letters and emails were sent to Judge Bailey's attention from those in support of Haynes. Bailey ignored them all. He couldn't care less what those outside the courthouse thought. What the jury decided mattered most. He felt that in this case justice was served.

Wesley Haynes did not speak at the sentencing.

When asked about the fate of the reggae star?

"With good behavior and time already served, Haynes could be out of prison in five years," one of his attorneys John Goodman told reporters both in Jamaica and the U.S.

"What happens now to his Madison Square Garden performance?"

Asked one curious Wesley Haynes' picture-on-a-large–placard supporter.

"I guess he will find a way to make it up to his fans, said another of his attorneys outside the Mandeville courthouse."

Haynes was quickly whisked away in a police transport vehicle to the General Penitentiary. As the vehicle sped away one female onlooker in her 50s yelled out:

"They should have tried him in America. The Jamaican Prison System is the worst. The stray dog in the street will probably get better treatment!"

While most on occasion referred to that prison system as a hell house.

CHAPTER 15

Although imprisoned, Wesley Haynes' reggae music continued to burn in the hearts and souls of many. It wasn't long before his wife Britney was able to release a remix of his single CD, while Wesley Haynes remained incarcerated. This international release hit hard into the musical arena, creating a severe dent. Profits soared; many of his local fans, to them it seemed like he was right there performing for them in the clubs and restaurants in

Kingston and concert venues around the country. While others; conscious of the fact that Haynes was still incarcerated; waited in anticipation for those five to ten years to pass.

The band, not able to hang together without their leader fell apart. Mike the percussionist joined another band in Miami. Max the drummer performed in local gigs back in Jamaica while peddling and pushing narcotics on the side. Winston the bass guitarist became a bartender. Through it all they were happy in the fact that they still received royalties from the hit song *This Is My Time*.

THE YEARS WENT BY FAST with Wesley Haynes still inside the *Pen*. The 911 bombings of the World Trade Center were behind us. People were coming together on different fronts. Although on the other hand racism still left its scars, and in some cases still remained a sore. It was well known that the civil rights revolution of the 60s not only diluted racism but left an open wound still in need of healing. America still in need of racial healing had elected its first black president. On the other hand, Saddam Hussein, the president of Iraq was captured and killed. Christopher "Dudas" Coke, the drug king pin of Tivoli Gardens was extradited from Jamaica to the United States. People were caught up in the epiphany of going green. The age of "i" had emerged, giving birth to i-phones, i-tunes and most recently i-pads.

WHO SHOT THE SHERRIFF?

Hip-hop music was still taking a hard rap mainly from the religious sector. Even so, it still had dominance. China and other Asian countries had bought into the Hip-hop culture. Reggae music continued to evolve as even R & B singers and Pop stars like Rihanna were including that vibe in their musical portfolio. Prior, most Reggae artists were re-recording *covers* of famous R & B and Pop artists. Now even songs like *What Goes Around Comes Around* by Justin Timberlake has a reggae melody submerged within.

After almost 6 years since that ship laden with narcotics was found adrift off the coast of Port Antonio, Wesley Haynes was released from prison on the grounds of good behavior. He had heard about the changes in the world while inside the *Pen*. But now being on the outside of those walls sure put all those evolvements into proper perspective for the singer.

Conversely, Sherriff John Brown was still pompous as that night when he put Haynes in jail and vowed to pull the rug out from under the singer, and the day he testified in court deflating the singers' character. Brown remained a hero for bringing down Wesley Haynes in that narcotic trafficking investigation and trial, but although near retirement age of 55 he still worked for the Mandeville Police Department.

On the other hand, the way was paved for a strong comeback for Haynes whose remixed CD single was still doing well around the globe.

With the help of Britney, who always maintained a positive mental attitude throughout the entire ordeal, Wesley was able to convince his band members to return. They did, and in addition to their continued performances, they scheduled a studio session and recorded a second single CD A *Better Life Must Come;* which later laid the foundation for the recording of a complete album.

Wesley Haynes not only cleaned up his life and disassociated himself from narcotics but after the tour he returned to Jamaica and built a mansion and resided there in Mandeville, when not enjoying his other manor in Miami. Britney after a few months gave birth to their first son, Damien Michael Haynes. Wesley was happy to be a dad and create a lineage for his son Damien.

AS FAR AS Sherriff John Brown was concerned Wesley had laid the issue to rest. He had buried the hatchet. The locals kept on growing weed as most people had to keep up with their extravagant lifestyle. Now in Mandeville and most other Jamaican cities most parents struggled to send their kids to school owing to the high cost of education. Fewer and fewer men joined the police force because unless their parents had the money to provide them a quality education those types of jobs they never got. So there became a major glut in the police department.

To make matters worse, whenever there was trouble and the police were called in, most of those police officers never returned alive. It also became habitual for trouble makers to request police assistance regarding numerous fabricated incidents. When the police showed up the locals would block off the streets making it impossible for them to return without being slowed. Then they would capture, beat and kill the officers and confiscate their weapons.

Most of these criminals are known to have some of the most sophisticated eclectic forms of weaponry in their collection. Name the gun; if it has not already been confiscated they have it in their possession. When it comes to arsenal most of them are on par with the police, while others own weapons more sophisticated than most police departments not only in Jamaica but around the globe.

So because of a shortage of police officers, most veteran officers maintained their tenure with the police force in Jamaica. So did also, Sherriff John Brown!

CHAPTER 16

Early one Friday night in August Sherriff John Brown and Deputy Charles were in separate parallel parked cars near an intersection in Mandeville. Both drivers' windows were partially closed as both officers conversed with each other from car to car.

In the interim, the light turned yellow and a black speeding luxury vehicle unable to stop ran the yellow light which suddenly changed to red as soon as the vehicle reached the crosswalk on the other side.

WHO SHOT THE SHERRIFF?

The two Sheriff cars not waiting for the traffic signal to change took off in pursuit of the motorist.

Sherriff Browns' car ahead of the pack now with flashing lights and sirens is in chase of the eluding motorist. Deputy Ron Charles car follows suits with flashing emergency signals. Finally, the luxury vehicle stops and waits on the right shoulder.

The two men dart out of their vehicle with guns pointed towards the idle SUV. As both men got closer to the parked vehicle, two rounds of gun shots in quick succession cut them down to the ground from through the vehicle's rear windscreen. The luxury vehicle takes off in speed leaving Sherriff Brown and his deputy Ron Charles bloodied and lifeless on the street. The vehicle races unaccompanied through the streets of Mandeville.

Hours later, the Mandeville police department with sophisticated weaponry combed through the streets of Mandeville in search of the killer and runaway driver. They were in search of their number one suspect Wesley Haynes who was on Sherriff John Brown's all - time wish list.

Later detectives along with police units arrived at the crime scene. Moments later they surrounded Wesley's house in Mandeville. Like the S.W.A.T police they move in. Since there was no vehicle parked in the driveway, some of them occupied that space in take down style. They demanded Haynes' surrender while displaying their state of the art weaponry. There was no response. So they broke down the front and rear door simultaneously.

They entered the house in that same take-down style. Evidently there was no one at home. After perusing through the house they recovered a gun in Wesley Haynes' bedroom dresser. They were later able to determine Haynes as the registered owner of that firearm which they confiscated.

Still they continued searching through Mandeville looking for the singer. People fearing for their lives got out of their way. If Haynes was hiding under a rock in Mandeville they were determined to find him. The officers kept their hand on the trigger; ready to shoot in an instant. Wesley Haynes was nowhere to be found.

The aggressive news media picked up the story and ran it every which way they could. The newspaper headlines read:

Who Shot The Sherriff?

Sherriff John Brown and his Deputy Gunned Down After Traffic Stop.

Even before Haynes was confronted regarding the shootings not only were the police at the Mandeville station accusing him of the shooting deaths but the word on the street was clear: *Haynes Shot the Sherriff.*

At the time of the shootings no one had heard gun shots go off, a silencer could have been used as detective sources close to the crime later suspected.

WHO SHOT THE SHERRIFF?

AFTER THE SHOOTINGS it later became known that an elderly man and woman Doris Weeks and her husband Claude Weeks were returning home from church. They had just welcomed in the Sabbath with one of their church members and done some praying on her behalf. On their way home from dropping off the church sister, they passed the two parked police cars on the roadside. Then the wet bloody street connected to the two bodies lying up ahead.

"Oh my Gosh!"

Said Doris,

Claude saw what she saw and pulled over to the side of the road. They stepped out of their car and noticed the two uniformed officers looking lifeless. They called 119 and waited for the police to arrive. Moments after that call, several police officers converged on the scene. The couple explained to the officers what they had seen as they drove up the street from church. The officers took their statements.

Still Doris and Claude were taken in to the station for additional questioning by Detective Paul Stevens and Detective Mike Jones. Realizing that they had no connection to the crime the couple were apologized to, and then, released.

Meanwhile, police continued to search Mandeville looking for Haynes and the vehicle involved in the crime. Because of the huge amount of glass found at the crime scene it was evident the getaway vehicle incurred a busted windscreen. Mandeville Police visited several automobile glass repair shops questioning workers about recent glass repairs. Even so, there was no information which could be linked to the crime.

Like a thumb print everyone has an opinion and most were not afraid to voice it. Most felt that Haynes shot the Sherriff and his deputy because of their pursuit of him. The search also expanded into Kingston where the singer lived and performed on a nightly basis. Tired police officers worked on rotation. Officers from other cities pitched in to help in solving this crime dilemma. The look on the faces and in the eyes of most police officers in Mandeville said that they were in dire need of rest and recuperation.

"Mandeville had a few years prior hosted the Haynes drug trafficking trial which sent Haynes to jail but it was not prepared to deal with, and endure, the turmoil of this crime."

According to one Jamaican TV reporter,

There was some merit to this as they were working with a tired, understaffed unit. Additionally, many locals were reluctant giving up any information regarding the shootings. Bearing in mind, the same Sherriff was involved in seeing Haynes go to prison a few years prior. Recruiting from other police stations on a Friday night in Jamaica wasn't the easiest thing to have happen. With that Friday being a pay day period most were out splurging a portion of their *dough*. Most police stations needed who they had on staff and some to help keep a lid on weekend crime. With the continued shortage of policemen in Jamaica, this was not easy ordeal for most police stations to give up their key players. A few stations nearby obliged anyway.

A glass expert Sam Chang was brought into the crime lab. After recycling the glass and reassembling it by laying out the tinted windscreen on an adhesive surface it was determined the vehicle used in the shoot-out was an Infiniti SUV. Wesley Haynes also owned a vehicle in that SUV league which fitted the description!

Many questions were left unanswered as they had not yet caught up to the singer and his whereabouts.

CHAPTER 17

The manhunt for Haynes continued in Mandeville and its surrounding areas. "Just a glimpse of the vehicle involved would make it so much easier on manhunt operations and the investigation. Better yet, the license tags would pull this whole mystery together or ultimately, the culprit(s) turning themselves in would suffice," Says the lead detective Paul Stevens to his understudy Mike Jones.

WHO SHOT THE SHERRIFF?

It wasn't long before corroborated reports poured in to the Mandeville Police Department. Haynes, it was reported was last seen at MO Bay airport preparing to board a plane bound for the U.S. His wife Britney and their son Damien were with them along with two bodyguards.

"Now the evidence seemed to be weighing in against the reggae artist as many, including members of the growing prosecution team, learned that Haynes had possibly killed the Sherriff and his deputy, and fled the country."

Says one TV reporter on the station's late night news,

"Though many questions remained unanswered: Why did Haynes leave his gun behind in the drawer of his bedroom dresser? What happened to the vehicle which was involved in the crime? Where was Haynes at the time of the murders? Did he commit those murders?"

As the Jamaican Police began to put information together an APB was placed on Haynes, they at least wanted him to help them solve this puzzle with some yet unanswered questions. Later after an extensive search of the MO Bay airport facility, based on a tip from a parking attendant who recognized Haynes' license tags while filling out his nightly report. The SUV registered to singer Wesley Haynes was recovered at the airport parking garage.

Police who discovered the black Infiniti SUV sensed that apparently it was not the vehicle involved with the shooting deaths but leaving no room for errors they had it towed and impounded for the possible collection of blood spots sample, hair and other DNA evidence.

Did they hit the homerun about Haynes' involvement now that they had recovered his vehicle? They were getting closer and felt strongly he had fled the country. Even so, they had not yet found Haynes and his vehicle didn't have a busted windscreen. If he did carry out those double killings why he didn't turn himself in and avoid an ambushed manhunt, many police officers queried.

UPON ARRIVING IN MIAMI and watching the late evening news the singer says he learned for the first time, that Sherriff Brown and his Deputy were gunned down, according to one TV reporter who stalked Haynes at the airport before he got inside his limo.

Haynes knew that many fingers would be pointed at him. Still watching the news as it unfolded he realized that the Mandeville Sheriff Department and other Jamaican law enforcement agencies were looking all over Jamaica for him. He was most stunned when he saw the tow truck towing his SUV to the pound and the pictures of what looked like S.W.A.T. Police surrounding his Jamaican home.

Later that afternoon, Haynes met with his newly formed legal team in Miami to discuss and be advised. His legal team advised him there was nothing to worry about when they heard his alibi. After all, the burden of proof rested in the hands of Jamaican law enforcement and as of yet they had no evidence to arrest the singer.

According to the autopsy performed on Sherriff John Brown and his deputy Ron Charles, results indicated that Brown died at 8:33 PM that evening and Charles at 8:35 PM two minutes immediately afterwards. Both men died from single gunshot wounds.

According to the record, the flight bound for Miami took off at 9:30 PM that same evening. If Haynes was the motorist who committed those murders based on the timeline he would not have enough time to abandon the vehicle and get to the airport to catch his flight. Bearing in mind that the distance between Mandeville and MO' Bay where the murders occurred is at least 65 miles. Therefore, it seems farfetched linking Haynes to the crime based on the timeline.

Could his wife Britney be a coconspirator? Even if his wife drove the SUV to the airport and he took a cab after supposedly killing the two officers, the singer still would not have made it there on time? He would have missed the flight. How about his two bodyguards who accompanied him on the trip to Miami? Could they have carried out the murder and driven to the airport in a Dodge Viper? Would they have made it there on time to catch that flight after going through tight airport security? Would Haynes leave his gun at home and travel with one bodyguard? Even if he did so, the other bodyguard would undoubtedly be able to catch that flight after cleverly getting rid of the still unrecovered getaway vehicle. Detectives at the Mandeville station had too many questions and very few answers.

Additionally, in support of Haynes' alibi a spokesman for the commercial airline issued a statement claiming that the flight from MO' Bay airport to Miami International Airport left on time at 9:30 PM and there were no delays and the Haynes family was on board. Weighing the evidence the prosecution felt that there wasn't enough evidence stacked up against Haynes to carry out an arrest.

Mandeville's Police Department was enraged with the prosecution's decision; they nonetheless, still felt that Haynes was their man.

Consolatory, on the part of Wesley Haynes after such great news; with enhanced security protecting him and his family he continued living as he chose. Except he chose to remain tight lipped when questioned by the media about his involvement in the double murder.

Britney in strong support of her husband figured that apparently someone tried to frame her husband knowing that the word was out that he had always had a running with Sherriff John Brown. Could someone else be raining on his hit parade? She queried.

Haynes' other band members joined him later that day at his Miami home, in support of his presumed innocence. To them their lead singer and friend said he was innocent of the alleged murder charges and that mattered most.

It was later learned that the bodies of both fallen officers were cremated and some ash stored at the local court house in Mandeville. However, two separate funeral ceremonies were held to mourn the loss of the Jamaican born, Sherriff John Brown and his deputy Ron Charles.

Many mourners were in attendance.

In the interim, Jamaican Law Enforcement pulled the registration profile of every registered Infiniti SUV on the island of Jamaica. A task force was sent out to inspect these vehicles and question the owners. Many drug dealers who owned the same make and model made concerted efforts to ensure their vehicle was free of narcotics. Nothing turned up to support any evidence related to the crime. They later agreed the vehicle used in the shootings could have been unregistered.

CHAPTER 18

Wesley Haynes and his band resumed their tour amidst much controversy that he was responsible for the murder of Sherriff Brown and his deputy Ron Charles. Although, Haynes was a suspect, according to sources close to the Mandeville police. The Police had to back off from arresting him as they realized they didn't have sufficient proof to convict the singer of the crimes in question. How they wished, though, that they could locate the vehicle which was involved in the murders! The Jamaican Law Enforcement departments launched an island-wide search for that vehicle. They searched Alleys, Trenches, Ravines, Junk Yards, Chop Shops, Auto Repair Shops, Tractor Trailers, Construction Sites, Abandoned Lots, Rivers, Lakes, Beaches, Land Fills, Garages, Forests, Parking Lots, Ships, Burial Sites, and anywhere else they thought a vehicle could be hidden. Even so, they came up empty-handed.

Meanwhile, in New York City Haynes and his band arrived at Madison Square Garden accompanied by an armed entourage. On the outside many jubilant supporters wore T-Shirts reading: *Who Shot The Sherriff?*

Inside, the concert was about to begin shortly. The announcer came on stage. He was dressed in an all-white outfit. This sold-out crowd was eagerly anticipating this event, which had been rescheduled, after almost six years.

"Ladies and gentlemen!"

Said the announcer, who continued after the huge applause,

"This is not only the evening we've been waiting for, but an event that the New York Tri-state area could not do without for much longer. Stand on your feet and gave a massive Big Apple welcome to the reggae artist of our time Mr. Wesley Haynes."

WHO SHOT THE SHERRIFF?

The announcer departed and the lights went down fading to black. The all black members band took their position dressed in black. As Wesley walked out, also dressed in all black, the lights came up. He looked like he was: *Coming to America.*

Everyone was now on their feet. Wesley and his band kicked off the event with a mixed reprise version of *This Is My Time.* The crowd went nuts.

Britney joined them on stage also dressed in black as the band segued into a *cover* song. The audience, from the nose bleeds sections, to the floor engaged in a wave as the performance continued. It was a spectacle to watch. They had waited over six years for this event and Haynes and his band delivered spectacularly.

As the musical vibes continued to reverberate, the entire Madison Garden crowd was rocking and dubbing to the sweet reggae beat. The band played their best and the singers gave it all they had. The place was in a musical frenzy. After a very entertaining performance the music faded on to the last song for the night. The crowd remained on their feet waiting for more. They started another wave interlude in anticipation.

Wesley looked across at Britney and together they looked behind at the band. They cranked a 3 minute reggae medley to close the event. New Yorkers had an evening they would never forget.

WHO SHOT THE SHERRIFF?

News spread swiftly about the success of the New York City Madison Square Garden concert. Many New Yorkers were still talking about this amazing event days afterwards. More so in Mandeville, Wesley Haynes' home town, even if they had not been physically present to experience the event they jubilantly commented on it.

CHAPTER 19

It was obvious the prosecution was not done with Wesley Haynes. Pressured by the Sherriff's associates they kept on digging for substantial evidence, enough to make an arrest of the singer. With so much speculation surrounding that crime, but also mainly because of Haynes' alleged involvement in these murders, it seemed as if the powers to be were secretly planning to go ahead and arrest Haynes anyway even if he was just a suspect.

WHO SHOT THE SHERRIFF?

That was the dialog circulating amongst the police in Mandeville.

On the other hand, they felt as though they were walking on thin ice or egg shells if this whole thing were to backfire on them. Wesley Haynes could get back at them for making an unlawful arrest. He had enough money to drag their entire department through the mud.

ALMOST A MONTH LATER, the murders, still unsolved and the authorities looking for a possible break in the case, the phone at Detective Paul Stevens office rings. It's Lloyd Matthews from the ballistics department. He is ecstatic.

"Hey Paul, I think we have something we could use to attach Wesley Haynes to those murders."

"Great. Lay it on me!"

Says Paul Stevens,

"According to our ballistic findings, the bullets which claimed the lives of Sherriff Brown and Ron Charles matches the handgun retrieved from Wesley Haynes' house on the night of the murders."

"Great! Put that gun in the vault and keep it there."

Says Stevens,

"BTW, fax me your findings ASAP. Thanks."

Paul Stevens walks out of his office stoked. He feels like they have made a dent in the case. He just needed the confirmation.

WHO SHOT THE SHERRIFF?

IT IS NOW ONE MONTH AFTER the murders of Sherriff John Brown and Deputy Ron Charles. The crime lab seemed like they had turned over a *double six*. The detectives close to the case were awaiting ballistics confirmation. Detective Paul Stevens teams up with Mike Jones and together they had in the meantime flown to Miami and interviewed Wesley Haynes for the first time.

Both detectives met with the singer at his home. Britney, his wife was present and also participated in the meeting.

When asked where he was on the night of August 12 when Sherriff John Brown and his deputy Ron Charles was murdered, Wesley said that he was at the airport heading to Miami. Britney concurred. He was then asked what time the plane departed; he said it left at 9:30 PM sharp. When asked why was he flying to Miami. Haynes mentioned that he and Britney were scheduled for rehearsals prior to performing at the Madison Square Garden Concert.

"Why didn't you take an earlier flight?"

Questioned Stevens,

"It only takes a few hours flying to Miami from Jamaica. I figured once we arrived we'd get some sleep and wake up the next morning ready for rehearsals the next day."

Haynes was asked if he knew Sherriff John Brown and Deputy Ron Charles. Haynes told the detectives that he was pulled over almost a decade ago and arrested by Brown. Continuing, Haynes added that he saw Brown again during his trial more than 5 years ago. Sherriff Brown had testified at the trial.

About the Deputy Ron Charles? Haynes said that he had no prior knowledge of Deputy Charles; he had never met him.

Jones presented photographs of the victim Charles to Haynes. Haynes looked at it and said: "I never met him, never seen him."

The detectives then asked Haynes if he owned an Infiniti SUV.

Haynes answered,

"Yes."

Detective Jones produced a picture of a black Infiniti SUV and asked Haynes if that looked like his automobile. After carefully looking at the picture Haynes said:

"That looks like my automobile."

Stevens then asked Haynes if he had owned a hand gun.

"Yes,"

Replied Wesley Haynes.

"And where that gun is now?"

Asked Stevens.

"Gun's at my home in Mandeville."

Stevens continued,

"Your gun is registered?"

"Yes. It is."

Responded Haynes.

"Why don't you travel with it versus leaving it behind?"

Stevens inquired.

"I don't want to forget it's in my possession while going through airport security. It belongs at the house. Plus, I've made it a habit to let my bodyguards worry about security when I am on the road. That's what they get paid to do."

Jones asked,

"Mr. Haynes did you shoot Sherriff John Brown and Deputy Ron Charles?"

At this point they get poised to squeeze a confession out of him.

"I did not,"

Replied Wesley Haynes,

"What if DNA collected at the scene proved otherwise?"

Stated Paul Stevens,

"I don't think anyone would be crazy enough to plant my DNA at the crime scene."

Said Haynes,

Jones sent a text message to headquarters to find out if there was any new information on the missing vehicle. There was none. Without it they realized they were only standing on one foot in regards to arresting Wesley Haynes. With Haynes vehemently denying his involvement with the double murders, the detectives had only one piece of evidence to go on – the hand gun. But they still needed confirmation from ballistics that the bullets matched Wesley Haynes' gun.

Once again Stevens produced the picture of the gun. Although there was no evidence placing Haynes at the scene of the murders the detectives were willing to throw as many curve balls they could to get a strike out.

"I must inform you that the bullets which took the lives of both officers were recovered and bullets fired seemed to match your gun."

Stevens added,

"Seemed? I don't see how that is possible. I never shot those guys,"

Says Haynes.

The detectives asked him if he would be willing to provide finger prints and hair samples and accompany them to the station to do so. He agreed. Haynes supplied the officers with prints and hair sample at a Miami Police Station.

In the interim, both detectives conferred that Haynes was their prime suspect even though they didn't have sufficient evidence stacked up against him. They were persistently, methodically building a case against Haynes. Judging body language and whatever they could glean from Haynes that showed a guilty reaction.

In the interim, the police department in Jamaica had received the faxed confirmation on the ballistics test and their boss informed detective Jones via text that they needed to arrest Haynes based on the limited amount of evidence against the singer. They felt that if the timing of death was miscalculated Haynes could have done it. Plus, the bullets matched.

With the timeline still up in question, they articulated privately that he could have used a car that looked like his Infiniti. Then drive his car to the airport and park it there. Maybe he didn't want any DNA findings from blood drops from the victims, so he chose to switch cars. Apparently he knew where the Sherriff placed his speed trap. So he sped through that street, encouraged the chase stopped his car and when the officers proceeded to investigate, he shot both of them and hid the car.

Additionally, because the bullets matched the gun, they felt strongly up to this point that it was him who had committed the murders and no one else.

Moments later they read Haynes his rights and arrested him based on the ballistics test. Haynes was held in custody with possible extradition to Jamaica in order to stand trial for both murders and facing death penalty if found guilty.

CHAPTER 20

M eanwhile, the legal minds in Mandeville were busy putting their prosecution team together for this high profile trial. Judge Roger Carmichael was appointed to rule in the case. Carmichael was younger and had recently replaced the senior former judge Christopher Bailey who had previously sentenced the singer to 10 years in prison and had recently lost his battle with pancreatic cancer.

WHO SHOT THE SHERRIFF?

Most locals felt that Haynes would get a fair trial with a new judge on the bench. One who was in his age group and probably a little bit more understanding of the nature of the murder case.

It was a given that many Jamaicans were still upset about the guilty verdict in the Wesley Haynes narcotics trial almost a decade ago. Many still debated the case at Barber Shops and other establishments, claiming he was wrongfully convicted.

Even so, in the case at hand, Jury selection was set to begin in a few days. The overseas press was gearing up to embark on Jamaica for this high profile trial of the Jamaican reggae artist. Was the largest city, in the parish of Manchester in the county of Middlesex in the island, of Jamaica ready for all this? In the eyes of most nationals it was. However, the wavering prosecution team saw it differently and opted out of having the case tried in Mandeville, fearing that the singer would walk scotch free. There was discussion of a Kingston held trial but the political ramifications could be devastating for the ruling political party if Haynes won the case. Haynes had developed strong political ties in Kingston and was revered by the entrepreneurs in that town who were strong supporters of the opposition party.

They considered New York but with most of the Jamaican population abroad living in that city they imagined seeing almost a quarter of a million demonstrators outside the courthouse in protest. New

York turned down their proposal stating that the singer had no ties to the Big Apple. Not even a physical address.

Miami where the singer lived, owned property, bought a house for his parents, and was held in custody was their next option. After days of negotiations, Miami agreed and jury selection in that city was underway.

News soon spread rapidly in Jamaica that the case would be tried on U.S. soil. That decision not only paved the way for several days of rioting from a rambunctious simmering local posse, but several police officers lost their lives during the protests. Mandeville supporters of Haynes demonstrated wearing their *Who Shot The Sherriff?* T-Shirts in gold, black, and green colors.

One TV reporter asked a black T-Shirt wearing supporter: "Why are you demonstrating against the trial being held overseas?"

The middle aged woman answered,

"He is like a modern day Bob Marley and we believe he is innocent. He was boarding an airplane at the time of the murder. It could not have been him who did it. That Sherriff had always been giving him problems but I don't believe he did those murders. I really don't think he would get a fair trial in America. They don't understand our complicated legal and political system."

WHO SHOT THE SHERRIFF?

When a member of the prosecution was asked by the same reporter about that woman's viewpoint:
He responded,
"That is for the Judge and Jury to decide if he is guilty or not. We believe he is guilty as he had every reason to commit the murders. Once again we will put our faith in the Judge and the Jury."
The demonstrations which erupted in Mandeville started on Friday morning at the crack of dawn and lasted throughout the weekend at sundown. The three day protests ended as many of Wesley Haynes' supporters had to return to work on Monday. So by Sunday's sunset the numbers of people parading the streets of Mandeville began to dwindle.
On Monday morning the news broke as a different judge Monica Finley a native of Kingston and living in Miami was appointed to the bench. She was dubbed as a no-nonsense judge with a 90% conviction record. Her 10 year tenure on the bench in Miami was immaculate according to most prosecutors. About her they jokingly articulated: "There's a method to her madness." They loved that *guilty ratio*.
The majority of the Jamaican prosecution team stayed in tack for the now overseas trial.
Five hours was spent the following day selecting the nine member jury made up of five men and four women. The Jury consisted of two African American male, one African American woman, two Caucasian male, two Caucasian women, one Hispanic male, and

one Asian woman. With the jury selection completed, the trial was set to begin on Wednesday inside the Miami courthouse.

Wesley Haynes elected to go with a new defense team from the one which represented him in his narcotics trafficking trial. He selected Collin Mattes to head up his defense team, a fellow Jamaican from Kingston who lived in and had been practicing in Miami for 7 years.

Many Jamaican reporters and other civilians interested in the case by this time had already arrived in Miami for this all important trial. Many hosted Garage sales and some Tenement Yard sales in order to fund the trip. Some stayed with relatives while others stayed at hotels and motels. The U.S. government was very supportive in granting visas to those involved with the trial.

CHAPTER 21

It was now Wednesday morning and the trial was set to begin. The enormous crowd which gathered outside the Miami courthouse was made up of: many moonlighting lawyers, fans of Wesley Haynes, non-supporters, divorcees, bored housewives, single women, teachers, firemen, engineers, sculptors, painters, entertainers, writers, entrepreneurs, cab drivers, retirees, farmers dressed in coveralls, newspapers editors, journalists, TV news channels along with their personnel, clergymen, ex-cons, barbers, politicians, street vendors, off-duty police officers and even people who had never met the singer or heard of him before that day.

Many of them tried to crowd into the small courtroom. Only a handpicked few were allowed in. Those who stayed outside seemed as if they had left their problems behind and just wanted to be there to find out firsthand: *Who shot Sherriff John Brown and his Deputy?* Who pulled the trigger had now for months been the gossip worldwide and the residents of Miami were about to find out, *whodunit?* The crime, in which the singer and former narcotics dealer, Wesley Haynes was being charged. Of which if found guilty the singer could face the death penalty and be killed by way of lethal injection.

OPENING STATEMENTS WERE first delivered by the lead Prosecutor James Tolliver. In those statements to the jurors, he said the singer and former convicted narcotics dealer had struck the jack pot from his solo CD hit song and he decided to invest it in the booming marijuana industry which led to his downfall and not only did he blame the Sherriff for his demise, he shot and killed the officer along with his deputy.

According to Tolliver,

WHO SHOT THE SHERRIFF?

"Sherriff John Brown had been a veteran Sheriff in Mandeville for over thirty-five years and did not tolerate *bad boys* and drug dealers. Sherriff Brown also assisted in the investigation of Wesley Haynes which later convicted the singer for narcotics trafficking."

Tolliver also told the jurors that Haynes not only dealt drugs but he had on one occasion eluded Sherriff Brown during a traffic-stop through the streets of Mandeville. He said that although Brown caught him speeding on that early Saturday morning, he did not cite the singer. And, that even though he suspected him of using narcotics, he only searched his car, arrested him and took him to the station to provide a urine sample. Haynes was released the next day after bail was posted. Charges were however later dismissed.

Sherriff Brown, Tolliver said was a good man who didn't deserve to die. He kept drug dealers off the streets of Mandeville!

But during the address to the jurors, Collin Mattes for the defense stated that during a cross examination of Wesley Haynes, it was revealed that the singer, though he felt vindicated by Sherriff John Brown who was like a thorn in his side, Haynes decided to let sleeping dogs lie. He said Haynes had forgiven him.

Mattes emphatically told the jurors that according to his alibi Haynes the defendant was not in Mandeville during the time of those two brutal murders.

WHO SHOT THE SHERRIFF?

"Wesley Haynes was on a plane with his family bound for Miami during that timeline. A timeline which will prove the defendant is not guilty of these murders."

Haynes he said was scheduled to meet with his band members for rehearsals in Miami prior to their Madison Square Garden Concert to benefit AIDS victims.

Additionally, he let the jurors know that even though the singer had spent over five years in jail, he was released under good behavior. Haynes, Mattes added, had totally cleaned up his act and transformed himself into a model citizen working to help victims stricken with HIV aids.

"It takes a model citizen to forgive his enemies – Haynes did. Wesley Haynes decided not to fret because of evil doers. No wonder many of his supporters dubbed him as a modern day Bob Marley."

Said Mattes,

BEFORE THE TRIAL BEGAN, however, Haynes, with his wife Britney by his side told reporters, he was happy with the jury selection and felt that they would give the trial their best in an unbiased way.

The morning first opened up with Haynes in very high spirits. He was laughing and cutting up with his lawyers along with his band members. At one point he was seen kissing his wife Britney on the lips. He came to the trial dressed like a king, in a sharp looking black double breasted suit, a stripe shirt and a killer power tie.

In his opening address to the jurors, Collin Mattes also introduced Haynes as, "The singer of our times." At this point the defendant stood up, did a modest profile and relaxed back in his seat. As the proceedings began, he took out his pen and pad and started taking notes. He listened intently to the statements being made, glancing peripherally at the jurors to see their reactions.

Mattes reiterated to the jurors that Wesley Haynes was innocent, and had no connection with the dual homicide.

But Tolliver reminded them that Sherriff John Brown and Deputy Ron Charles were shot and killed and that the whole purpose of this trial was to find out who did it. He told them that he expected them to convict Haynes and nothing short of it. He also reminded them: not only did Haynes have several running with the law but he also disliked Sherriff John Brown.

Additionally, spending five years in prison could have generated enough venom in the singer to want to take Sherriff John Brown's life and anyone else associated with him.

Tolliver concluded by emphasizing:

WHO SHOT THE SHERRIFF?

"Wesley Haynes deserves to be punished for these crimes of injustice. It is no miracle that the death penalty is in place."

CHAPTER 22

The following day the court reconvened with Ryan Mundell who handled the autopsy. After being sworn in, Mundell in his testimony explained the cause of death. Mundell states that the gunshot wounds to throat of Sherriff Brown and to the head of Deputy Charles were the cause of the officers death. Mundell showed PowerPoint slides detailing the position of the bullet wounds on the bodies of both officers. During his picture-slide presentation he used a rule to draw attention to the throat area of Sheriff John Brown where that fatal bullet entered. He further explained that the bullet lodged in the upper vertebrae of the spine.

Mundell also mentioned that the Sheriff might have had a chance to live at least a bit longer if the bullet's impact had not severed his windpipe, disallowing the flow of oxygen to his lungs. As he continued to show these grotesque pictorial accounts Wesley Haynes was busily engaged at scribbling notes on his notepad and showed signs of sympathy on behalf of the Sherriff.

Mundell then showed slides of the bullet wound evolving from the gunshot to the head of Deputy Charles. With the same ruler he again pointed to the middle of Charles' forehead where the bullet entered. He further stated that the bullet went through the brain and lodged in the back of the deputy's skull. Mundell was questioned by both Collin Mattes for the defense and James Tolliver for the prosecution in regard to the timeline of these deaths. He informed both men that Sheriff John Brown died at about 8:33 PM that evening and Deputy Ron Charles around 8:35 PM.

Judge Monica Finley ordered a small 15 minute recess and then continued the hearings with Detective Paul Stevens taking the stand.

Stevens testified that he and detective Jones were called to the crime scene that night, a few hours after the murders possibly occurred. He stated that when he arrived he interviewed an elderly couple, who apparently called 119, stating that on their way home from church they saw what looked like an accident. They added that they got out of their car to see if someone needed an ambulance or CPR. At that point they saw the two officers lying there dead along the roadside.

The couple said that they figured that the officers had been shot as their bodies seemed pierced, one in the neck and the other in the head. They also claimed that they smelled sulfuric fumes like gun powder. It then was confirmed in their minds the men could have been shot.

We wanted to believe the couple but had to do our duty so detective Jones and myself had both of them transported to the police station. There we later questioned the couple more extensively and released them.

We felt that the couple did not commit these murders based on autopsy reports we had just received. The time of deaths just determined by the autopsy indicated that the deaths could have occurred between 8:30 PM and 8:35 PM.

While at the crime scene we made it a high priority to glean whatever evidence we could. The fresh broken glass at the scene indicated that the shooter could have fired the bullets through the back windscreen because a mini antenna was found amongst the broken glass. We collected the fragments of glass along with the two guns still held tightly in both officers' hands and delivered them to the crime lab.

The coroner was called onto the scene by detective Jones, and the bodies were later transported to the hospital.

That same night we visited Wesley Haynes' home. Haynes was listed as a prime, possible suspect because of his previous running with Sherriff John Brown. We were also informed he could be dangerous because of his prior narcotics associations and his entourage of bodyguards who worked for him so we went in with not only backup but with a strong police presence.

At his home we recovered a gun which after ballistic tests linked his gun to the bullets that have been determined to have claimed the lives of the Sherriff and his deputy on that fatal night.

More than two weeks ago after interviewing Wesley Haynes at his Miami home, we decided to fingerprint him and acquire hair sample. We didn't have enough to proof to arrest him then. We later received confirmation on the ballistics and then arrested Wesley Haynes and charged him with the murder of both officers.

Judge Monica Finley asks the lawyer of the defendant if he has any questions for detective Paul Stevens.

"Yes your honor," says Mattes.

Mattes, confers with Haynes then stands up.

"I apologize, your honor."

"Next time counselor, be sure to ask my permission before conferring."

Says Finley,

"I will your honor."

Mattes responds.

Mattes approach and address,

"Detective, your name is Paul Stevens is that correct?"

"Yes."

Responds Stevens,

"And you are an officer at the Mandeville station?"

"I am."

"And you just swore to tell nothing but the truth?"

"I did."

"How long have you been with the Mandeville Police Department?"

"I've been with the department for twelve years."

Stevens responds,

"How long have you known Sherriff John Brown?"

"For as long as I've been working at the Mandeville station."

Responds Detective Stevens.

"How would you describe the *man* who you have known in a working environment for twelve years?"

"Objection!"

Says Tolliver,

"Sustained,"

Says Judge Finley,

"Do you know Mr. Haynes?"

WHO SHOT THE SHERRIFF?

"No I don't."

"When was the first time you met Wesley Haynes prior to this trial?"

"I first met Haynes at his Miami home, when detective Jones and I interviewed him before arresting him."

States Detective Paul Stevens.

"Were you aware that the singer Mr. Haynes and Sherriff John Brown were at war with each other?"

"Objection your honor!"

Says James Tolliver, on behalf of the prosecution,

Objection sustained says the judge.

"Have you ever heard Sherriff Brown say that he is going after Haynes and he will bring him in to be sautéed like Escovitch fish?"

Detective Stevens fumbles,

Objection your honor this is tampering…

"Objection overruled. Answer the question detective Stevens,"

Says the judge.

"I did hear mention that Haynes was on his wish list but it could have been from a fellow officer. I don't recall hearing that statement directly from Sherriff Brown. I also did not hear the Escovitch fish marinating analogy."

"So you did hear something to that effect from one of your fellow officers?"

Asks Mattes,

"Yes. But I am not sure who said it."

"So Wesley Haynes' name was a *station word* in the green room, the smoke oasis, the early morning breakfasts, on the beat, the firing range, the stake outs, and in meetings at the Mandeville Police Station?"

"Objection your honor!"

Says Tolliver.

"Sustained,"

Says the judge.

"When did you consider Haynes a suspect, at the time of the murder or during the interview?"

"Haynes has always been a suspect we just didn't have enough evidence to make an arrest. Not until we ran the ballistics on his gun and later interviewed him regarding his alibi, was that confirmation received regarding the ballistics test."

Says Stevens,

"At what time did you visit the Haynes' home after the murder?"

Asks Mattes,

"It was around 10:35 PM on the night of the murders."

"Was it before 10:35 PM or closer to 10:45PM?"

It was closer to 10:35 PM."

"No further questions your honor,"

States Mattes as he takes his seat.

The Judge looks over at the prosecution team.

"Mr. Tolliver?"

She says.

Tolliver responds,

"I have no questions your honor."

"Detective Stevens you may step down,"

Says Judge Finley.

Finley hits the gavel and continues,

"This court is now in recess. We'll reconvene in thirty minutes."

Haynes closes his notepad and moseys outside with his wife and the rest of the defense team.

It was beginning to seem that whenever things heated up in the courtroom, Jude Finley would take a break so everything can simmer down before she continued with the next witness. Her mindset was to keep an orderly court room and not allow tempers to flare as things got out of hand.

CHAPTER 23

When the trial reconvened that afternoon Jude Finley invited Sam Chang, a crime lab expert with glass and metal suaveness to the witness stand. Chang began by stating his credentials as being actively involved with that area of criminology for over 15 years. He also said that it was very unusual to collect evidence from the rear windscreen. Mostly it's the front glass or front windows which get damaged in a vehicle gunshot related incident. Usually in an incident like this the front windscreen gets shattered because a gunshot is fired in a face to face manner, unless it's a drive by shooting, then the glass on the front door doors tends to get blown out. He further said that the tiny antennae found amongst the shattered glass, was a huge indicator that the glass was from the shattered rear window of the vehicle.

Chang also said the glass on the ground contained no tire marks so it could not have been the front windscreen, unless the vehicle moved in a parallel direction which is highly impractical. Also meshed into the glass fragments he was able to discover sulfuric fumes and smoke residue. Chang explained the tedious process of recycling the glass and to make the pieces fit like a jig-saw puzzle. Then he explained how he glued the fragments of glass back together again using *CrazyGlue*.

Chang walks over and removes the windscreen from its paper wrapping.

Mattes the defense lawyer approaches the table and takes in a good look at the windscreen. On the windscreen there are two holes. Chang indicates that the two bullets fired from inside the car went through those holes. Wesley Haynes takes written notes while he soaks up the information. In his imagination Haynes sees the windscreen as one which looks identical to his automobile.

Jude Finley says,

Mr. Mattes you may cross-examine the witness.

Mattes approaches.

"Great job Mr. Chang I can only imagine how much effort it took to put those pieces of glass back together again, every splinter has to be in place.

"Thank you!"

Says Chang.

Mattes continues,

"Is it possible to determine at what time the shots were fired through that piece of glass?"

"I am afraid there is no way to determine the time of bullets impact through the glass."

Says Chang,

"So, Mr. Chang what is the purpose of reconstructing a piece of glass if one cannot tell the time of impact, through it?"

Asks Mattes.

Objection,"

Says Tolliver.

"Objection overruled,"

Says Judge Finley.

"Sir, the main reason for reconstructing the glass fragments into a whole piece of glass is to be able to determine the make and model of the vehicle used in committing a crime when that vehicle involved in the crime is missing and not part of the crime exhibit."

Answers Sam Chang,

"No further questions."

Says Mattes,

WHO SHOT THE SHERRIFF?

"Mr. Tolliver?"

Says Judge Finley.

Tolliver approaches,

"Mr. Chang, your work is commendable."

Chang acknowledges.

Tolliver continues,

"In your analysis of the windscreen were you able to determine the tenure of the tint job?"

"Yes sir! The tint was done recently. The way the glass loosely attached itself to the tint is a clear indication that the tint job was still new. The tint job had to be done within the last three weeks to a month before the incident as the glue was still mending with the glass. It was a high grade tint - durable. The type they use in limousines."

Mr. Chang, in your findings were you able to determine who got shot first in this brutal incident?"

"That was one of the first things we looked at while putting the pieces of glass back together. The first bullet pierced the windscreen on the left. Ironically that bullet did not remove the windscreen. But the second did."

Chang points to the hole inside the windscreen on his PowerPoint illustration.

Chang continues,

"According to our analysis that bullet struck Sherriff John Brown who was approaching on the left side of the vehicle and towards the gutter. The second shot obviously, which came through the right of the windscreen completely detached it from its holding. Once again because of the way the windscreen was dislodged we were able to find other samples like pieces of hair and car fragrances."

"What scent were those fragrances?"

"A pina colada scent."

"What other evidence was found on the dislodged windscreen Mr. Chang?"

Asks James Tolliver.

Mr. Chang continues,

"We were able to retrieve fingerprints as well."

Wesley Haynes and Mattes exchange a glace initiated by Haynes.

"Thank you Mr. Chang. At this time I have no further questions."

James Tolliver returns to his seat.

"Mr. Chang you may step down."

Says Judge Finley.

CHAPTER 24

The Judge next calls Phyllis McPherson another crime lab expert to the witness stand. McPherson is a tall and beautiful African American woman. An expert with hair samples and works in the crime lab in conjunction with the Mandeville Police Department. McPherson was sworn in.

"Counselor you may proceed with your cross examination of the witness."

Says Judge Finley to Collin Mattes,

Mattes approaches,

He sizes-up McPherson. A scientific expert, employed by the city, and called by the prosecution. He visualizes this as an uphill climb knowing from experience that these types of witnesses are almost as the Good Book. Plus when Mattes looks around at his table there were no experts present except for the church couple. How he wished he had some full-fledged experts on his side.

He moves closer to the stand almost in the witnesses' space. Meanwhile James Tolliver is looking at him thinking what is this moron doing?

"Hello Miss McPherson, how are you today?"

"I am doing great,"

Responds Phyllis McPherson,

"I've noticed you've been involved in a few trials before this one. Is this trial of any major significance to you?"

"Objection!"

Says Tolliver,

"Objection sustained!"

Says the judge.

"How long have you been working for the crime lab Miss McPherson?"

Asks Mattes.

"I have been doing this kind of work for the last fifteen years. I have now worked a total of seven years with this particular crime lab in Jamaica."

WHO SHOT THE SHERRIFF?

Says McPherson,

"Miss McPherson you are aware that millions of hair samples are similar, don't you? Plus in most cases hair samples can only determine the race of an individual?"

Phyllis McPherson feeling the pressure responds promptly,

"While that is possible, a carefully studied DNA could in most cases link that offender to the crime."

Responds McPherson.

"Did you pick up these samples yourself from the crime scene or were they delivered to you?"

Tolliver looks across at Mattes and shakes his head thinking: *where is he going with this one now? Should I object again? I'd rather not. This might seem like the prosecution is losing grips on the case.*

"The crime lab maintains a high level of integrity and trust with the detectives on the way evidence is collected and delivered to the lab."

Collin Mattes probes,

"Based on your findings would you conclude that the hair sample collected by the detectives on that night when the two Sheriff officers were gunned down in Mandeville matches that of the defendant Wesley Haynes?"

"It is not a 100% match but at least 75% which in my experience I would say probable,"

States Phyllis McPherson.

"How probable?"

Asks Mattes.

"Quite probable.

"And you feel that a 75% quite probable is enough to convict someone?"

"Sir those are our findings,"

Says McPherson.

"No further questions,"

Says Mattes as he returns to his seat.

"Mr. Tolliver!"

Says Judge Finley,

Tolliver approaches,

"Miss McPherson thanks for all your hard work at the crime lab. May I ask how many pieces of hair did you examine based on evidence provided by the Mandeville Police?"

"We looked at two pieces of hair."

"Were they all the same in texture and color?"

Asks Tolliver,

"No sir, they were all different,"

Responds McPherson,

"How different?"

"They were both from the black race but different colors. One was jet black and the other was brownish."

"Were any of these dyed or artificially colored?"

"No sir. They were original."

"No further questions."

Responds Tolliver, who before he takes his seat glances across the way at Mattes as if to say: "Wesley

WHO SHOT THE SHERRIFF?

Haynes is going down. You can bank on it. Heck yes I'm like his new Sherriff, nothing he plants is going to grow. We are going to make that soil toxic. I'll watch as he gets electrocuted."

Wesley Haynes senses Tolliver's angle, trying to attach him to the crime.

Judge Finley strikes the gavel with authority, claiming:

"This court is in … recess! We will resume in 15 minutes."

CHAPTER 25

A drug dealer named Marcus Davis and currently serving time for drug trafficking, drug possession and having an unregistered gun in his possession was brought in by the prosecution to testify against Wesley Haynes. The prosecution thought that by getting him to gather some dirt on Haynes, they might have a chance to squeeze a conviction out of this case. After being sworn in, Marcus Davis testified that Haynes, prior to his narcotics arrest controlled most of the marijuana traffic up down the Caribbean Coast. He said Haynes supplied him weekly with at least 100 pounds of *chronic marijuana* back then. He also said that the ship which went adrift was loaded with a shipment, part of which was heading his way in Miami. Davis claimed that he paid Haynes for the narcotics in advance, also the shipping charges, which was very expensive.

According to Davis, that shipment obviously never arrived. He never got the weed and did not receive a refund from the dealer – Haynes. Davis said when he asked Haynes about the goods. Haynes told him to go to hell, and that the ship had been captured by Sherriff John Brown and dry docked at Port Antonio.

Davis further said that Haynes told him during that conversation how Sherriff Brown was always raining on his parade and that one day he was going to dry up those angry clouds.

Davis said he also asked Haynes how he was planning on getting rid of the *Sherriff* knowing that he was the most powerful Sheriff to ever wear a badge in Jamaica. Davis said Haynes responded: "according to Jimmy Cliff *Time will Tell, Time alone will tell.*

Collin Mattes approaches the witness stand intending on questioning Davis' credibility.

"Mr. Davis are you here today of your own volition?"

"I'm not. I was requested to be here. Because I had done business with Haynes."

"Mr. Davis, I understand that you are currently serving time. Is that correct?

"Yes I am,"

Says Davis,

"Is your testimony against my client part of a deal to reduce your sentence?"

"Objection!"

Yells Tolliver.

"Your honor may I proceed?"

Requests Mattes,

Some conversation residue ensues amongst court attendees including Tolliver and Mattes

"Order in court!"

Yells Judge Finley.

"Counselors, if this type of behavior continues in my courtroom I am going to have to reprimand both of you. Objection is overruled!"

Continues the judge.

"Mr. Mattes please continue."

"How many years is this grand appearance taking off your 15 years in prison sentence for drug trafficking and the possession of an unregistered firearm?"

"None. I volunteered after being asked to do this because I felt that justice should be served in the shooting death of Sherriff John Brown and Deputy Ron Charles."

Says Davis,

"A few minutes ago you swore to tell the truth, isn't that right?

WHO SHOT THE SHERRIFF?

States Mattes,

"I'm all for the truth. I have nothing to hide."

Says Davis,

"How much are you getting paid to do this?"

Asks Mattes,

"I am not here for the money."

"What are you here for then?"

"Justice."

"Justice...?"

"I have no further questions your honor,"

Says Mattes.

IN THE INTERIM, news broke globally that Wesley Haynes song *A Better Life Must Come* had just been nominated for the Grammys. Radio stations were playing his song over and over again. Finally his name was back in the news in a positive light. Commuters in New York, Boston, Chicago, Washington DC, Seattle, Utah, France, London, China as well as other cities and countries were now not only talking about the Haynes' trial but they were bopping again to his music. In the minds of his fans this timely nomination would possibly sway the minds of the jury to a no conviction.

On the other hand Haynes' non supporters were still opposed and queried as to why other songs instead of Haynes' weren't nominated for the Grammys? They claimed that Wesley Haynes has been charged with the murder of two law enforcement officers and should not have been given such public celebratory accolades. Plus he faced the death penalty in these charges if convicted.

Before the reconvening of the trial, the following day after the Grammy nomination news hit, Judge Finley informed the jurors in a closed meeting that people were attempting to try the case in the media. She also informed them that they were, however, the only ones entrusted with the outcome of this case.

The Hispanic woman juror and one Caucasian member were not present for the meeting. It was earlier brought to the judge's attention that the two jurors weren't feeling well and would not be continuing the trial.

Judge Finley informed the other jurors that the two members of the jury would not be continuing because of ill health. Also that the court will be adjourned for one day until those jury replacements were made.

The other seven jurors were happy to be away from the courtroom for an extra day. Although some of them would rather continue with the same core of jurors who were selected prior to the trial.

On the other hand, some felt it would be good to bring in some new blood facilitating fresh aura in the jury box.

As for the prosecution as well as the defense: This was a much needed break to cool tempers and get a fresh start when the trial continued in two days.

CHAPTER 26

Wesley Haynes, while in prison entertained frequent visitors. His wife Britney was the most popular. She would visit several times a week in addition to being present next to him inside the court room. His visitors were always well screened. The palladium surrounding the singer was always very tight. Now that the news about his Grammy nomination surfaced, security around him was beefed up instantly by prison officials.

Haynes, not sure what his fate was going to be. He couldn't see how he got entangled in this web. Even so, he depended on his defense team to make the right decision regarding his fate in the trial.

While in prison he kept very much to himself except when he had visitors. He didn't trust anyone on the inside. He knew that those who visited him were well-screened.

Now with enhanced security he felt protected within those walls.

His cell, #11 adjacent from #12 and #13 colored shinny light gray on the inside with a window which served only as a skylight. His two neighbors, Reggie occupied # 12 and Nigel in # 13. Reggie in his mid-30s was on death row for killing five police officers in South Beach. While Nigel, now in his 50s was serving a 25 to life sentence for a series of rapes. Nigel had already served 12 years of that life sentence and seemed not to give a darn about being paroled.

Every morning Nigel, before the breakfast alarm sounded would call out the names of his rape victims: Cynthia, Thelma, Mavis, Maria and Isabella as loud as he could. Though he had been sent to the hole on several occasions for that type of behavior he didn't care. Apparently calling out their names was his therapy. He had done it so often at this point the wardens sensed that he was immune to the hole so they ignored his boisterous, insane attitude. Although at times they did put him in mainly to set precedence.

WHO SHOT THE SHERRIFF?

Many inmates said that Nigel was still possessed with these women after being incarcerated for almost two decades. Some saw him as an outright lunatic. Other inmates at Westview were also constantly sent to the hole. It seemed like to them a dark revolving door.

Most of the prison incidents which warranted this punishment stemmed from fights, loud noises, threats and stealing. The men who smoked were only allowed to do so under supervision in a room known as the smoke oasis.

While at the smoke oasis most inmates kept their cigarettes back at their cell under lock and key. No one trusted anyone. That's how the relationship was at Westview.

Breakfast was served at 7:00 AM daily. If you missed it you didn't get any. The ration made up of scrambled eggs, grits, and watered down coffee was served 7 days a week.

Lunch and dinner was the same meal except that it was served at different times and sometimes it was pork and at other times chicken. It comprised of a scoop of steamed rice, a piece of broccoli or carrot, with a small portion of mashed potatoes and a piece of meat. If you didn't eat pork you would enjoy a meatless meal on the days it was served. Most people ate chicken. The ones who claimed they were Vegan or Rastafarians received no substitute. To wash the meal down watered down limeade or water were the only two choices. Some viewed the limeade drink as urine. Most inmates preferred water which they called H20. So at mealtime H20 was highly favored over limeade.

Most inmates at Westview prison shared a bunk bed which was cemented to the wall except for these three inmates, Wesley, Nigel and Reggie.

The exercise grounds, securely gated and the size of almost three basketball courts was their community sanctuary. The gossip, the sports news, the presidential elections, the gas prices although none of them were currently driving a vehicle, how the stocks traded was one of the favorite topics, even though no one invested or had money to do so. If something happened or was going to happen it was aired here. Women are known to gossip a lot but most of the men at Westview had them beat.

Some inmates played Frisbee while others played dominoes, monopoly and basketball. Some of the biggest cheats in monopoly were housed at Westview. When it comes to basketball, the Piston Bad Boys of Detroit could not step in the shoes of the ten players usually allowed to grace the court.

After every basketball game it was like a bloodbath. You had to come ready to play and be prepared for fights either during the game or afterwards. There were no officiating referees so no one fouled out. Those not ready for the game of basketball played some other game or watched from the sidelines.

WHO SHOT THE SHERRIFF?

Yes. On the inside it was very much a *dog eat dog world* as those who were in had no problems confronting another prisoner looking for a fight. So when that inmate retaliated, a fight ensued. As a result they would be reprimanded and were sent to live a more constrained prison life. Like it's said: *misery loves company*. Inside those prison walls it was an actual fact!

Wesley Haynes, though he loved basketball feared to thread. He had enough dirt thrown at him on the outside so he avoided any confrontation within those walls. To him there was enough rivalry in the courtroom. So he would resort to his cell and do push-ups in order to keep fit. The inmates referred to him as Mr. Goody Two Shoes. To Haynes it didn't matter. He wanted out of there.

Lockdown was held twice a day at 4:00 PM – 5:00 PM and then at 10:00 PM. This was not a much celebrated event by the inmates at Westview. You could tell by their body languages that something was getting ready to happen which annoyed the heck out of them even before the command was given.

Inmates such as Nigel found it despicable and overly structured. But that was life within those walls. They made a head count and filed reports during the first event. Afterwards they had dinner.

Some people including Wesley Haynes went to their cells or to the library, others just hung out playing ball, shooting Frisbees or enjoying an intense game of dominoes or monopoly.

At 10:00 PM the day was a wrap, followed by lights being switched off. When that announcement was made by the Warden, it was official, it was understood. Even if *Henny Penny* or *Ducky Lucky* showed up and said that the sky was falling, it was a wrap! Those two characters would be looking up to the skies all by themselves.

Wesley did not enjoy this lifestyle. Although it was a lot better than conditions he had endured while in Jamaican prison. Where it was understood, even the stray dogs on the street were treated better than the prisoners in Jamaican jail. He couldn't see himself living like that for much longer.

"Something had to change," he told himself.

As was stated earlier, his quiet time was spent reading and writing. Including doing pushups to keep himself fit. His small library included a *Bible* along with motivational literature. He read a lot from the "Proverbs," "Ecclesiastes" and "Revelation." The *Book of James* he completely soaked up.

At nights before the "lights out" command. He wrote lyrics to songs and meditated before hitting the sack. Haynes knew that his fate was in someone bigger and greater than himself. He held on tightly to the idea that *late in the midnight hour God was going to turn things around.*

WHO SHOT THE SHERRIFF?

Haynes had watched the news and read the papers not only about the status of his trial, although he tried avoiding the repetitious drama in which he was involved. He was there seeing it unfold LIVE before his eyes. Even so, his name had surfaced all day in the news on two fronts, so he indulged in keeping in the know.

Plus not only were people talking much about his Grammy nomination, most were reveling in it. He couldn't avoid soaking up all the press. Although behind those walls at Westview he kept a very low profile.

On this particular night, he was not only excited about his Grammy nomination, but was happy about the adjournment; giving him a break from the court room the following day.

On the other hand he wondered how the new jury replacements were going to affect his trial. He tried not to worry about it too much but the whole thing was consuming him.

Haynes questioned his own fate in that if the new jurors, who were on the outside, were looking in, for days. How he hoped they would not bring the mindset of his non supporters to the trial. Haynes wished they would have continued with the same jury even if he didn't know what verdict they would have aided in presenting to the court.

Newly replaced Jurors tend to want to try the case based on what the public is saying even if they are told not to, he envisioned.

"How could they after discussing a case with others not bring their opinions into the Jury Box?"

He questioned.

All in all he had to go to sleep to be fresh and ready for what in his mind was going to be a new day in the chapter of his trial. He didn't know what to expect except that there was going to be a different aura from inside the jury box. The warden passed by his cell and announced:

"Lights out!"

Haynes realized that the day was a wrap. Yet he struggled with the idea and finally forced himself to sleep.

CHAPTER 27

The trial resumed the following day on schedule. Defense lawyer Collin Mattes wanted a win for his client and nothing less than that. He sensed that evidence was lacking. So what do you do when evidence is lacking? You apply pressure on the opponent and get into the heads of the witnesses. Like in basketball when you smell a victory you put the other team under defensive pressure causing them to turn the ball over. That morning he in many ways showed up with his game face on.

Wesley Haynes showed up looking his best in a nicely tailored gray suit which looked like it was made for him. His dotted shirt appropriately complimented his new tie. Looking across at the jury box, there were nine jurors present.

He didn't want to treat this day as the day of the verdict knowing that a lot more witnesses were still in the lineup; his lawyer had hinted to him that it could be a long trial. Judge Finley had a history of dragging things out in addition to maintaining order and taking long breaks. She wanted it all delivered in her courtroom.

The jurors were poised. The view of the jury box was inescapable.

Wesley Haynes scanned it thoroughly for the demographical makeup. Not sure if that would have anything to do with changing the outcome but the thought was there and he was subconsciously holding on to it. He noticed however that an East Indian female juror and a Philippine woman replaced the two sick jurors.

"Let the show begin!"

He said in his mind. He pulled out his pad and readied himself. How he wished today was the finale.

Sitting next to her man was Britney Haynes, dressed to the nines.

WHO SHOT THE SHERRIFF?

At nine o'clock on the dot court was called into session. Judge Monica Finley took the stand and announced the jury replacements. Judge Finley looked like she had tanned deeper with a possible spa treatment during her one day off from the bench. She was upbeat.

Finley then addressed the jurors:

"Ladies and gentlemen of the court I must let you know that the two new jurors have already been briefed and are very much up to speed on the unfolding events in this trial. With that said I would like to call our next witnesses to the stand."

In no time the next witnesses were introduced, the first for the defense: A couple, Claude and Doris Weeks, who were the first to arrive at the crime scene after both the Sherriff officers were gunned down.

The couple looked like they were dressed in their church best outfits. The oath was read and taken. Mattes, invited by Judge Finley to cross examine the next two witnesses, approaches.

"Mr. and Mrs. Weeks, good morning! I know this is not your conventional environment but an innocent man's fate is at stake in this trial and as a witness that fate is also in your hands. You apparently were the first people on the scene on that night when two Officers, John Brown and his deputy Ron Charles were gunned down on that Friday evening of August 12th. Take the jurors back to what you witnessed on that late evening."

WHO SHOT THE SHERRIFF?

Claude speaking for the couple address:

"Thank you, Mr. Mattes. You are correct this is not where we choose to be. My wife Doris and I are pastors of a Seventh Day Adventist church in Mandeville, and would rather be out caring for the sick and afflicted but this is where, we are called to be.

We live a few blocks from the church and also from where the shootings occurred. Normally we don't take that route home but on that evening we gave, a sister in Christ who was going through some tough times, a ride home after praying with her at the church. After dropping her off, we took what you might call the "back roads" to our home. It was the eve of the Sabbath our desire to get home was a priority so we could be fresh and ready for church the next day.

We saw two parallel parked Sheriff cars along the roadside. The vehicles looked suspicious because none of their parking lights were on.

"Why would two police cars be parked in that manner?"

Doris asked.

I told her something must be wrong and I wondered if someone stole their cars.

As we continued up the street, we saw two bodies on the ground over on the side of the street. I was going to drive past them. But my caring wife asked me: What if they need an ambulance or CPR? In the same breath she reminded me of the story about the Good Samaritan. So I pulled over. There was broken glass and blood on the street. When we looked closely at the two men it really sank in that they were two Sheriff Officers, by their uniforms and badges. Their guns were still in their hands.

The smell of gun powder was thick in the air, which added up to the bullet wound in the neck of one officer to the left and the other wound in the head of the other officer on the right. They were lifeless. We realized that there must have been a shooting which left them dead.

Doris reminded me that, that was a crime scene, so to try and not touch anything. She also questioned as to why the police has not been here on the scene.

"They haven't taken care of their sheep."

She said,

"There are two missing sheep, where is their shepherd?"

I wanted to leave, for me it had been a long day. Plus we had to get home, get enough rest in order to officiate in church the next day. Doris reached into her purse, grabbed her cell phone and called 119 to report the incident. We both felt obligated to stay until the police arrived. So we tarried a little bit longer.

When the two detectives, Stevens and Jones arrived we told them what we had seen. They questioned us as to who we were and where we were going. We told them the gospel truth. They put us in the back of their car. As we waited other police officers and coroners showed up. The two detectives continued collecting evidence, taking pictures and sweeping up pieces of glass.

We felt like it was time to leave but wanted to be obedient citizens. We were later driven to the station in Mandeville by detective Stevens and Jones. At the station we were questioned some more before we were released."

Inside Judge Finley's court room it is so quiet that you can hear a pin drop!

"What additional questions were you asked?"

Questions Mattes of the defense,

"Questions like: Do you know Sherriff John Brown and Deputy Ron Charles?"

"Do you own a gun?"

"Have you fired a gun before even if at a shooting range?"

"Do you own a second car?"

We told them no and that we do not own a second car.

They asked if we owned a second car what make and model would it be.

I told them that we weren't materialistic. Doris at this point was more tired than I was and said:

The Word says: "lay up for yourself, treasures in heaven … "'We don't need a second car.'

It was then that they released us and drove us back to our car.

"No further questions your honor."

Mattes takes his seat.

"Counselor Tolliver?"

Says Judge Monica Finley,

"Mr. Weeks in your recollection: What time did you first arrive at the crime scene?"

Asks Tolliver,

"We were there at 9:30 PM."

Says Mr. Weeks

"How soon did the police arrive?"

Asks Tolliver,

"They were there 15 minutes later at 9:45 PM."

Says Mr. Weeks,

"No questions for the witnesses your honor."

Finley strikes her gavel.

"This court is in recess, lets reconvene in 15 minutes."

Britney looks at Wesley, he looks at Mattes. They then look across at the jurors.

CHAPTER 28

The trial hearings resumed for yet another day and Britney Haynes, the wife of defendant Wesley Haynes was called to the witness stand. Judge Monica Finley invites Mr. Tolliver lead member of the prosecution team to cross-examine Britney Haynes another defense witness. Britney is sworn in.

Mr. Tolliver approaches,

"Mrs. Haynes, good morning."

"Good morning."

WHO SHOT THE SHERRIFF?

Say Britney Haynes,

"This must be a horrendous task being here every day with your husband who is on trial for murdering Sheriff John Brown and Deputy Ron Charles. You understand the due process I am sure."

Britney gives a partial smile.

Mr. Tolliver continues,

"You understand the oath which you have just taken, right?"

"I do."

Says Britney,

"And you do swear to tell the truth?"

"I do."

Says Britney,

"Tell us about your husband."

Wesley pays attention as if he doesn't want to miss a word.

"Wesley and I have been married for almost 8 years. We've been together two years prior. Wesley has been a leader in everything; he has done including track and field. My parents were very skeptical when they realized we were serious about each other. I must tell you he absolutely shocked them.

Wesley is a good family man, a great husband, a great dad. He did not commit those murders of which he is accused. He was with me and our son Damien at the airport in preparation to boarding a plane to Miami when those murders were committed. This is a complete waste of our time dealing with a crime which we absolutely have no connection to. This is not due process this is processing dues and we are paying with our time."

Britney breaks down in tears.

She draws everyone in.

Britney finally composes herself.

"What time did you arrive at the airport Mrs. Haynes?"

Asks Tolliver,

"Wesley, our son Damien and I arrived at the MO' Bay airport at about 8:30 PM,"

States Britney.

"Were you wearing a watch at the time Mrs. Haynes?"

"Yes, I did."

Says Britney,

"Did you check your watch when you arrived at MO' Bay airport?"

Asks Tolliver,

"I didn't."

"Why not?"

Asks Tolliver.

'We take this trip to the airport regularly. It takes us about an hour to get to the airport from our house. We left our house at 7:30 PM."

Says Britney,

"At what time did you and your family board the aircraft?"

Asks Tolliver,

"We boarded at 9:10 PM when everyone else did."

"What time did that flight depart?"

Tolliver questions,

"The flight departed at 9:30 PM,"

States Britney.

"What was the purpose of that Miami trip?"

Questions Tolliver,

"We were visiting Miami for rehearsals prior to a Madison Square Garden Concert,"

Responds Britney.

"What was the tenure of your rehearsals?"

Tolliver asks,

"We rehearsed for three days,"

Responds Britney.

"Your event was scheduled for May 27th Memorial Day according to the New York Times. You still had a two day window."

Asks Tolliver,

"We took our son on a tour of New York City."

Responds Britney Haynes,

"Thank you. No further questions."

Says James Tolliver as he returns to his seat,

"Mr. Mattes, do you have any questions for Mrs. Haynes?"

States Judge Finley,

"Yes your honor."

Mattes addresses Finley as he approaches the witness,

"Mrs. Haynes, you have been through a lot during the last eight years. You have raised your son while your husband was imprisoned. Here you are going through yet another trial. How do you handle all this?"

Asks Mattes,

"I believe in God and I believe in my husband Wesley. He's got many rivers to cross but this is his time,"

States Britney Haynes.

That statement hits Mr. Mattes emotionally.

"Thank you Mrs. Haynes. I have no further questions."

Mattes ambles back to his seat.

CHAPTER 29

Three weeks including weekends had now elapsed since the trial began. Although many witnesses had already testified and been cross-examined that Monday morning found Wesley Haynes and his wife Britney, along with the court room regulars back in the courtroom of Judge Finley. After saying her good morning, Finley had Max Richards the band's percussionist called to the witness stand. The Judge then invited James Tolliver to cross-examine Richards a witness for the defense.

WHO SHOT THE SHERRIFF?

Richards was questioned about his tenure with the band. He was further asked if he knew Sherriff John Brown or ever met the Sherriff. Max Richards never met him or Deputy Ron Charles, so he told the court he didn't. When asked if he ever heard about Brown? Max said it was hard for people who lived in Mandeville not to hear about such a prominent individual unless they lived under a rock.

"You seem to have a great relationship with Wesley Haynes, the defendant. Have you ever heard him make any threats on Sherriff John Brown's ...?"

"Objection your honor!"

Yells Collin Mattes for the defense.

"Objection sustained,"

Says Finley, who continues,

"Mr. Tolliver I am warning you ...,

Tolliver continues,

"Have you ever heard any threats made by anyone in the band on the life of Sherriff John Brown life and that of Deputy Charles? Did you make any of your own?"

"No sir, I heard none and made none."

"Tell me about your Madison Square Garden Concert."

"Objection your honor, that question is irrelevant,"

Says Mattes.

"Counselor Tolliver what does that question have to do with the trial?"

Asks Judge Finley,

WHO SHOT THE SHERRIFF?

Collin Mattes is now on his feet.

"Your honor may I approach the bench?"

Says Mattes.

"You may,"

Says the judge.

The two counselors approach the judge's bench.

"Your honor, all I am doing is trying to determine the motive behind the defendant's trip out of the country, right at the time when the two murders were committed, with his gun linked to the crime."

"You may want to address your question differently counselor. We are taking an unscheduled recess for fifteen minutes. Please meet me in my chambers,"

Says Judge Finley.

"This court is now in recess for fifteen minutes."

The judge strikes her gavel.

Inside the chambers, judge Finley warned the two counselors about the importance of sticking to questions pertaining to the trial.

"We don't need to deal with all the irrelevant stuff. Not in my courtroom. Let's keep it professional and respect the juror's time."

Says Finley.

THE TRIAL RESUMED. That afternoon Detective Mike Jones was asked to take the stand, as a witness for the prosecution. Jones was the accompanying detective dispatched to the scene of the murders with his senior partner Detective Paul Stevens on the night Sherriff John Brown and Deputy Ron Charles were gunned down. He also accompanied Stevens to Wesley Haynes' home in Miami where they both cross-examined the singer prior to making the arrest. The jurors had heard from his partner Paul Stevens before, so did Wesley Haynes who readied himself by taking copious notes.

Judge Finley invites defense lawyer Collin Mattes to cross examine. Mattes asked Jones to describe what happened on the night of the murders.

Detective Jones talked about being called to the scene and not knowing what to expect. He stated that with the 119 call coming in relayed by a civilian who was at the scene where two Sheriff officers were gunned down, there was a degree of skepticism. Mainly because it was a common thing for civilians to make those kinds of calls and when officers are dispatched to the scene they realize that it was a hoax. By then it's too late as these officers are ambushed, robbed of their weapons and in most cases killed. He reiterated how frequent those crimes were. He said in his mind the callers could have been connected in some way to those murders also. So he expected the worse.

Arriving at the scene of the murders he and his partner questioned Claude and Doris Weeks an elderly couple who claimed they saw the bodies in the street on their way home from church and called 911.

Jones later showed pictures on PowerPoint slides of the evidence retrieved from the crime scene. Those graphics included the corpse of Sherriff John Brown and his Deputy Ron Charles, the shattered rear windscreen of the getaway car, glass fragments on the street, the tire imprints of the vehicle, the two parked Sherriff cars. Next Jones shows slides of Wesley Haynes vehicle parked at the airport parking lot along with it being towed, Wesley Haynes' recovered handgun and a wide shot of the crime scene showing the intersection, Sheriff cars and the gunned down officers.

Mattes asked Detective Jones:

"Detective Jones, at what point in your investigation did you feel you had enough evidence to arrest defendant Wesley James,"

Jones said.

"Upon receiving confirmation on the ballistics test."

"And when was that?"

"At the police station."

We asked Mr. Haynes if he would accompany us to the station for finger printing and hair sample. He agreed though we sensed he was uncomfortable. He was very nervous about the process. Plus we felt he was our man by his nervous reaction when we told him that the ballistic test connected his gun with the shots which claimed both officers' lives."

"No further questions."

Says Mattes as he returns to his seat.

WHO SHOT THE SHERRIFF?

Wesley Haynes' two Bodyguards were next called to the stand. The defense asked them about the timeline traveling form Montego Bay international airport to Miami on that night of the shootings. Both men confirmed a 9:30 PM departure from MO' Bay to Miami.

The prosecution then quizzed the bodyguards concerning Wesley Haynes' alibi. The guards re-confirmed they departed MO' Bay airport at 9:30 PM on that Friday night. Tolliver also asked if he had anything to do with the shootings of Sherriff John Brown and Ron Charles. Both men denied any involvement in the shooting and death of Sherriff Brown and his Deputy.

Another day in the trial was concluded as announced by Judge Finley.

CHAPTER 30

It was now Friday and almost two months into the trial would have elapsed. Without the getaway car, James Tolliver the lead prosecutor knew from the outset he had a legal challenge to face in this case. The lack of hard evidence against the defendant was factual. The only thing he had to go on really was the recovered handgun, and share speculation mixed with he say she say. But he was willing to fight to the very end. Death by lethal injection faced Wesley

Haynes if Tolliver was able to pull out this win for the prosecution. This high profile case would show him off as an elite prosecutor. Additionally, Tolliver was eager to see Wesley Haynes fry.

Tolliver had supplementary evidence like the hair sample which could have belonged to anyone else than Wesley Haynes. He had character witnesses who didn't care about dragging the defendant through the mud. He had some expert testimony which so far didn't hold much ground in the case. Although he had the possible murder weapon, the non-corroborating timeline, didn't put the defendant at the crime scene in the opinion of most.

How he wished the getaway car would surface at some point during the trial. Thanksgiving and Christmas had passed, as did the New Year. Still when it came down to hard evidence, Tolliver was not delivered any treats. The late breaking evening news stating the SUV believed to have been involved in the murders was spotted in a ravine was nothing but a hoax. The unregistered vehicle was checked out by Mandeville police officers and had a busted rear windscreen but that original back windscreen for the most part around the corners was still intact.

THE COURTROOM FELT AS if things were winding down. Just like the last two minutes in a basketball game. Except no one had yelled - two minutes!

WHO SHOT THE SHERRIFF?

Wesley Haynes sitting as usual next to his wife Britney and defense lawyer Collin Mattes showed signs of impatience although still ready to write.

The ballistics expert Lloyd Matthews was called to the witness stand and sworn in. Matthews had been recently appointed by the Mandeville Police Department and assigned to the case after the shooting-deaths of Sherriff John Brown and Deputy Ron Charles. He had previously worked for the Kingston police for 10 years. Matthews by far was the prosecution's star witness. He held the keys to unlock the only major piece of evidence thus far which could possibly connect Wesley Haynes to the murders – the handgun.

After the taking of the oath, Judge Finley invited defense lawyer Collin Mattes to cross-examine the witness. Mattes steps up in-front the witness stand.

"Good morning Mr. Matthews. It seems like you have been handed a very delicate assignment. One which could most likely determine if my client Wesley Haynes, who is facing possible death penalty, be convicted of the crimes of shooting Sherriff John Brown and deputy Ron Charles on the evening of August 12th.

Mr. Matthews, what process was used by your lab to determine if the bullets which killed both officers on that night were fired from the gun belonging to the defendant Wesley Haynes?"

"A basic procedure was followed where a bullet from the defendant's gun was shot into a tank filled with water. After that bullet was recovered it was viewed under a comparison microscope and determined it was a match."

Matthews responds,

"Did you perform the same test on the guns of Sheriff John Brown and that of Deputy Ron Charles?"

Asks Mattes,

"No. I did not."

Says Matthews,

"You did not? I can't believe this. Really? May I ask you why not? The two officers Brown and Charles allegedly died from gunshot wounds, two guns were recovered at the crime scene belonging to both men. Another gun was recovered from the defendant's home belonging to the defendant. You conducted ballistics test on the defendant's gun but not on the guns of Sheriff John Brown and Deputy Ron Charles. Why not Mr. Matthews?"

Asks Mattes, demanding answers,

"There was no reason to. I didn't think it was necessary. I had already discovered that the bullet matched the gun of the defendant."

"What type of gun was found on Sheriff Brown when he was shot and killed?"

"A Glock 38,"

What type of gun was found on Deputy Charles when he was shot and killed?

"A Glock 38."

What type of gun was found and retrieved from the home of Wesley Haynes on that same night.

Matthews responds,

"A 38 45 GAP"

"Same guns, Mr. Matthews,"

"That is correct,"

Says Matthews.

"My common sense would tell me if three guns are identical there is more than an 80% chance they could discharge the same bullet unless that gun had been reconstructed."

"Probably,"

Says Matthews,

"Probably or most likely?"

Asks Mattes,

"I would say probably,"

"Were any of these gun's reconstructed?"

"Not to my knowledge,"

"Mr. Matthews. Are you cognizant of a crime known as friendly fire?"

"Objection!"

States James Tolliver,

"Objection overruled!"

Says the judge,

"Your honor, I would like to propose that the court takes a recess so Mr. Mathews could complete ballistics evidence on the guns of Sherriff John Brown and Deputy Ron Charles."

Asks Collin Mattes for the defense,

"Objection to such a decision! This is an attempt by the defense to prolong this trial,"

States James Tolliver,

"Objection overruled."

Says Judge Finley,

"You honor, may I approach the bench?"

"Yes counselor you may."

Tolliver does.

"Your honor, the defense is trying to sway the minds of the jurors."

"Your honor how could I sway the jury? They have not yet deliberated the case. They have no hard evidence against my client except for those manufactured and hearsay. How could he not have done ballistics on the other two guns? Is this a ploy to convict my client?"

"Gentlemen you need a timeout." Judge Finley says to the two lawyers.

Judge Finley asks James Tolliver:

"Mr. Tolliver, how long would your witness take to return to the court his ballistics findings on both guns:"

"I have no idea, I could find out for you during a recess."

"Thank you let's get to work."

To the court the judge orders,

WHO SHOT THE SHERRIFF?

"This court is in recess for 15 minutes!"

During the break, Tolliver met with Lloyd Matthews. After a few made phone calls, Matthews determined it would take at least 5 hours to bring back to the court the necessary ballistics findings.

The court was called back to order. Judge Finley informed the court the trial would be adjourned until 3:00 PM that day. And when it did, they would continue with the cross examination of ballistics expert Lloyd Matthews.

LATER THAT EVENING the trial resumed with ballistics expert Lloyd Matthews on the witness stand. Defense lawyer Collin Mattes continues his cross-examination of the witness.

Mattes, continues and goes straight for the *jugular*.

"Mr. Matthews based on your recent findings is there any new discovery you would like to share with the Jurors?"

"After putting the guns of Sherriff John Brown and Deputy Ron Charles through the same ballistics test as was done for Wesley Haynes' gun. It was determined that those fatal .45 bullets were in close resemblance to those also fired from the officer's guns during the test. The mystery remains: How did all three men wind up with the same type of weapons?"

Mattes asks,

"Which of the bullets examined in your tests was the closest to the ones which killed both officers?"

"After the comparing of all five bullets under a comparison microscope, they all look similar."

States Matthews,

"No further questions your honor,"

Says Mattes as he saunters to his seat.

Haynes is taking copious notes.

Judge Monica Finley looks at Tolliver.

"Mr. Tolliver!"

Says the judge,

Tolliver approaches,

"Thanks for all of your hard work Mr. Matthews. In conclusion, based on your findings would you say that the defendant's gun is exempt as the possible weapon used in the murder of Sheriff John Brown and Deputy Ron Charles?"

"No. It doesn't."

Says Matthews,

"No further questions your honor."

Says James Tolliver returning to his seat,

CHAPTER 31

It was almost the end of the day. Several witnesses had been heard from. Defense lawyer Collin Mattes had just finished drilling the ballistics expert. The court room should have been due for a recess after that episode.

Judge Finley looked across at the clock on the wall at the rear of the courtroom, and then across at the jury. Mindful of those in that special box she didn't want to tire them out with all this explosive testimony at once.

WHO SHOT THE SHERRIFF?

"It has been a long trial thus far,"
Says Finley with empathy,
"We could leave our final witness for tomorrow but my gut instinct says we should get to the end ASAP. This would give our jury the weekend to prepare their early deliberation. With that said, I would like to invite Mr. Milton Rogers to the witness stand."
The court announcer echoes,
"The court calls Mr. Milton Rogers!"
Milton Rogers ambles his way from the rear of the courtroom to the front. He takes the oath and settles down in the witness chair. The judge calls Collin Mattes to cross-examine the witness no doubt leaving Tolliver to have the final swing at the defense's witness.
"Mr. Rogers good evening! Sir, tell us about your relationship with the defendant Mr. Wesley Haynes."
Rogers composes himself then proceeds.
"I first met Mr. Haynes over 8 years ago in Kingston. He was introduced to me by a dear friend Clyde Gumbs. Clyde was a patron at my restaurants for many years. He called me one afternoon and said he met a very ambitious gentleman, a singer with style-Wesley Haynes. He said Haynes had recently moved from Mandeville to Kingston. Clyde said that Haynes had worked for him, and besides being a talented singer he is very trustworthy.
Clyde Gumbs asked me if I would be willing to hire Wesley Haynes to perform at Michael's bar and Grill,

a restaurant which I owned. I then looked at my schedule and told Clyde I could use the singer on Thursdays and Fridays, and to have the young man give me a call so we can talk further.

The next day after lunch hour I received a phone call from Wesley Haynes. I told him I was busy for the next two days but I would love to have him come in so we could talk. He showed up on Monday afternoon, and after the interview we booked him for Thursday and Friday of that same week. He was excited and told me his girlfriend Britney was his backup singer and she would be accompanying him.

Haynes wowed the guests on both nights with his music. So I rebooked him for those nights every week. A few weeks later Max, Mike, and Winston, three band members joined them. It wasn't long before they blew up as their music caught on. So much that I had no choice but to turn many guests away on those nights, due to lack of space.

The rumor was out that one Sherriff John Brown from Mandeville was looking for Haynes to pull the rug out from under him. One night while entertaining some guest at Michael's, I saw a car pull up. The driver refused to valet park and blocked the driveway. The parking attendant called me over to intercede.

Out walked a man in street clothes. I could tell by the bulge in his waist he had to be armed. No sooner did he flash his Sheriff's badge.

WHO SHOT THE SHERRIFF?

He asked me if I was the owner. I said yes and how may I help you? He said he was looking for Wesley Haynes. Wesley and Britney had been gone for more than a week. So I told him they are not here. I then asked him who I should tell them stopped by. He said Sherriff John Brown. He asked me several times: "Are you sure you are not hiding them, because if you are, I will arrest you for obstruction of justice."

"I have no reason to hide anyone,"

I said.

"He asked me the same question again. I then told him I didn't think it was any of my business to relay the man's whereabouts. He searched through the crowded restaurant, displayed his gun and then left upset. I was later informed by one of my managers: that Sherriff Brown visited one of my other restaurants and arrested some innocent patrons."

Concluded Rogers,

"Have you been in contact with the defendant since that incident?"

"This is the first time I am seeing Haynes since his performance at *Michael's*. However, we've talked a few times during the last 8 years."

Mattes asks,

"What was the nature of those few sporadic conversations?"

"We talked about the hit parade - the progress of his music,"

Says Rogers.

WHO SHOT THE SHERRIFF?

"Was the Sherriff accompanied by other officers when he visited your restaurant looking for the defendant Wesley Haynes?"

"No he was by himself and as I mentioned carried a gun which he displayed,"

Replies Milton Rogers.

"What type of gun was it Mr. Rogers."

Asks Mattes,

"A Glock 38."

Says Rogers,

"Did he tell you why he was looking for Haynes or did he say that a warrant was out for his arrest?"

Probes Mattes,

"No he didn't."

"Did he leave you any of his contact information?"

"No he didn't,"

Responds Rogers.

"No further questions your honor."

Mattes says as he returns to his seat,

James Tolliver for the prosecution approaches the witness, Milton Rogers.

"Mr. Rogers, you claimed that you spoke with the defendant over the years. Were those conversations constant or sporadic? And who initiated those conversations?"

"We spoke sporadically. Sometimes I called and at other times he did. He's a busy man and so am I. All we did was touch bases."

Answers Rogers.

"Would you say once a month, twice a month or every day?"

Asks James Tolliver.

"More like twice a year."

"During those sporadic conversations did he say anything to you or did you ever overhear him say he was going to shoot Sherriff John Brown and his deputy or that he had killed both men?"

Questions Tolliver.

"Wesley Haynes never did."

Says Rogers.

"Mr. Rogers did you or anyone you know shot and kill Sherriff John Brown and his deputy Ron Charles?"

"No. I didn't and don't know anyone who did."

Says Rogers,

"Mr. Rogers, do you drive or own an Infiniti SUV?"

Asks Tolliver.

"No. I don't,"

Says Rogers.

"Did you know the late Bill Parsons?"

Questions Tolliver,

"Yes."

"What was your relationship with the late Bill Parsons, his posse and how did you fit in with the music industry in Kingston?"

Questions Tolliver.

"Objection!"

Yells Mattes,

"Objection overruled, answer the question Mr. Rogers."

Says Judge Finley,

"Bill Parsons was a patron of mine. He brought a lot of high profile clients most of whom were in entertainment to eat at my restaurants throughout Kingston. He liked our food and bragged about it to his peeps."

Responds Rogers,

"Was Bill Rogers a drug dealer?"

Asks Tolliver,

"Objection!"

Says Mattes,

"Objection overruled."

"That I don't know he never told me."

"What did he tell you he did for a living? I am sure he divulged."

"Parsons said he was a music producer. He was very well respected. That is the most I know,"

Says Rogers.

"No further questions."

Says Tolliver as he returns to his seat.

CHAPTER 32

The entire courtroom was in eerie as the trial now entered into the closing arguments phase. Although some felt like there should have been more to this drawn-out-almost-two-months of trial. Collin Mattes went first and went through a list of some of the high points of the testimonies presented by witnesses and said:

"Nothing has been presented by the prosecution to find my client Wesley Haynes guilty of the murders of Sherriff John Brown and Deputy Ron Charles. This has been nothing more than a case lacking crucial hard evidence. Again I ask: Where is the vehicle from which these bullets were fired? Which of the three guns recovered, was the one from which those two bullets were fired, that claimed the lives of Sherriff John Brown and his deputy Ron Charles?

Those all very important questions are still left unanswered. Men and women of this hard working jury, I know the matter rests in your hands to decide if the defendant Wesley Haynes is guilty or not guilty. I believe you will do a calculated job to return with a not-guilty verdict."

James Tolliver was the finale. Tolliver spent almost thirty minutes. He wandered on in his argument, going through what was said by the witnesses supportive of a guilty verdict. After which he gave his intelligent interpretation of justice and why the jurors should return with a guilty verdict. About justice Tolliver said:

"What is justice? Justice is fair, just, or impartial legal process. What then is justice when those who have wealth can buy their way out of a crime? What is justice when the opulent can get away with murder?

Innocent people lose their lives every day and those who are responsible for those deaths, if they are rich are often allowed to walk. This has to stop. We cannot progress when the guilty are allowed to go free. Our system is ruined from the ground up when it comes down to justice.

We've heard many testimonies during this trial. Two men of the law gunned down in cold blood on that fatal Friday night in August. It is your duty…"

James Tolliver stares across at the jury and continues, "To deliver justice in this case. Justice will only be delivered by a guilty verdict. As a jury, that climax rests solely in your hands."

The prosecution and defense both rested. Judge Finley gave the jurors until the following morning at 9:00 AM to return with a verdict. The jury retired that afternoon to begin their deliberation.

EVERYONE IS SITTING on edge in the court house except for the Jurors and the Judge.

Judge Finley

"Good morning ladies and gentlemen of the Jury. Have you reached a verdict?"

"Yes we have your honor!"

"Would the defendant please rise?"

Wesley Haynes stands.

"Will the foreperson please read the verdict?"

"Yes your honor."

On count one of the shooting and death of Deputy Ron Charles, we the jury find the defendant Wesley Haynes not guilty.

WHO SHOT THE SHERRIFF?

On count two in the shooting death of Sherriff John Brown, we the jury find the defendant Wesley Haynes not guilty.

Judge Finley says,

"The court is dismissed."

Britney grabs, hugs, and kisses Wesley. Collin Mattes waits for his turn to congratulate Wesley Haynes and does so to Haynes and his wife. Other Haynes supporters are jubilant not only in the courtroom but around the globe.

The crowd outside the court house in unison yells:

"Hip Hip Hooray, Hip Hip Hooray!"

CHAPTER 33

Much effort had been put into the well anticipated Grammys. Ever since Wesley Haynes received the Grammy nomination for his hit song A *Better Life Must Come*. The Grammys had been peppered with controversy as to why the song of a prisoner, an alleged murderer had been nominated for such a prestigious award. Many church organizations even though the song had a positive message had planned on boycotting the event.

WHO SHOT THE SHERRIFF?

The committee on the other hand, felt that no matter what, they were going to host the event. They realized history was filled with events in the past threatened by a boycott. They were not going to bend; they were not going to fold.

Wesley Haynes' song was still rocking the charts at number one.

It was Grammys night. Haynes had been found not guilty in the murder of Sherriff John Brown and Deputy Ron Charles just a few days prior by a jury of nine. Although many still had their doubts thinking he was the only one who could have done it. The verdict spoke differently.

The event was packed. Haynes supporters lined the streets wearing their *A Better Life Must Come* T-Shirts. It finally came down to the announcement of the winner.

Many at home were glued to their TV sets, supporters and non-supporters alike.

The host returned after the featured band did a number. In a very emotional state of mind, the host addressed:

"What is to happen will and in life there are no coincidences. This years' Grammys goes to Wesley Haynes for his song *A Better Life Must Come*. The entire room went into applause.

Everyone was now on their feet, applauding. The room was transformed from frenzy to pandemonium.

WHO SHOT THE SHERRIFF?

Lights, from the many cameras, were flashing everywhere.

Wesley and Britney Haynes graced the stage and the applause grew louder. Wesley accepted the award, gave it to Britney and took the microphone. Wesley's parents Megan and Sebastian, Britney's parents James and Christine, Rose Best–Parsons, Grace and Milton Rogers were all in attendance. How they cheered…,

"Thanks to an awesome God, they meant it for evil but He meant it for good!" Thanks to my wife Britney, our parents! Thanks to band members Max, Mike and Winston, mentors, the naysayers… Thanks, to the Grammys! This is indeed a better life!"

The singers holding hands returned to their seats.

The audience continued to cheer. Crowds on the streets cheered including those in foreign countries and different time zones. People at home watching the Grammys on TV were cheering. Radio stations phone lines were jammed with people calling in and requesting the song. The radio stations did, *let his music play*!

About The Author

John A. Andrews hails from the beautiful Islands of St. Vincent and the Grenadines and resides in Hollywood, California. He is best known for his gritty and twisted writing style in his National Bestselling novel - Rude Buay ... The Unstoppable. He is in (2012) releasing this chronicle in the French edition, and poised to release its sequel Rude Buay ... The Untouchable in March 2012.

Andrews moved from New York to Hollywood in 1996, to pursue his acting career. With early success, he excelled as a commercial actor. Then tragedy struck - a divorce, with Andrews granted joint custody of his three sons, Jonathan, Jefferri and Jamison, all under the age of five. That dream of becoming all he could be in the entertainment industry, now took on nightmarish qualities.

In 2002, after avoiding bankruptcy and a twisted relationship at his modeling agency, he fell in love with a 1970s classic film, which he wanted to remake. Subsequent to locating the studio which held those rights, his request was denied. As a result, Andrews decided that he was going to write his own. Not knowing how to write and failing constantly at it, he inevitably recorded his first bestseller, Rude Buay ... The Unstoppable in 2010: a drug prevention chronicle, sending a strong message to teens and adults alike

Andrews is also a visionary, and a prolific author who has etched over two dozen titles including: Dare to Make a Difference - Success 101 for Teens, The 5 Steps To Changing Your Life, Spread Some Love - Relationships 101, Quotes Unlimited, How I Wrote 8 Books in One Year, The FIVE "Ps" for Teens, Total Commitment - The Mindset of Champions, and Whose Woman Was She? - A True Hollywood Story.

WHO SHOT THE SHERRIFF?

In 2007, Mr. Andrews a struggling actor and author etched his first book The 5 Steps to Changing Your Life. That title having much to do with changing one's thoughts, words, actions, character and changing the world. A book which he claims shaped his life as an author with now over two dozen published titles.

Andrews followed up his debut title with Spread Some Love - Relationships 101 in 2008, a title which he later turned into a one hour docu-drama.

Additionally, during that year Andrews wrote eight titles, including: Total Commitment - The Mindset of Champions, Dare to Make A Difference - Success 101 for Teens, Spread Some Love - Relationships 101 (Workbook) and Quotes Unlimited.

After those publications in 2009, Andrews recorded his hit novel as well as Whose Woman Was She? and When the Dust Settles - I am Still Standing: his True Hollywood Story, now also being turned into a film.

New titles in the Personal Development genre include: Quotes Unlimited Vol. II, The FIVE "Ps" For Teens, Dare to Make A Difference - Success 101 and Dare to Make A Difference - Success 101 - The Teacher's Guide.

WHO SHOT THE SHERRIFF?

His new translated titles include: Chico Rudo ... El Imparable, Cuya Mujer Fue Ella? and Rude Buay ... The Unstoppable in Chinese.

Back in 2009, while writing the introduction of his debut book for teens: Dare To Make A Difference - Success 101 for Teens, Andrews visited the local bookstore. He discovered only 5 books in the Personal Development genre for teens while noticing hundreds of the same genre in the adult section. Sensing there was a lack of personal growth resources, focusing on youth 13-21, he published his teen book and soon thereafter founded Teen Success.

This organization is empowerment based, designed to empower Teens in maximizing their full potential to be successful and contributing citizens in the world.

Andrews, referred to as the man with "the golden voice" is a sought after speaker on "Success" targeting young adults. He recently addressed teens in New York, Los Angeles, Hawaii and was the guest speaker at the 2011 Dr. Martin Luther King Jr. birthday celebrations in Eugene, Oregon.

John Andrews is from a home of educators; all five of his sisters taught school - two acquiring the status of school principals. Though self educated, he understands the benefits of a great education and being all he can be. Two of his teenage sons are also writers. John spends most of his time writing, publishing books and traveling the country going on book tours.

Additionally, John Andrews is a screenwriter and producer, and is in (2012) turning his bestselling novel into a film.

See more in: HOW I RAISED MYSELF FROM FAILURE TO SUCCESS IN HOLLYWOOD.

Visit: www.JohnAAndrews.com

Watch For The Upcoming New Releases...

Coming Soon!

RENEGADE COPS –
CROSS ATLANTIC FIASCO

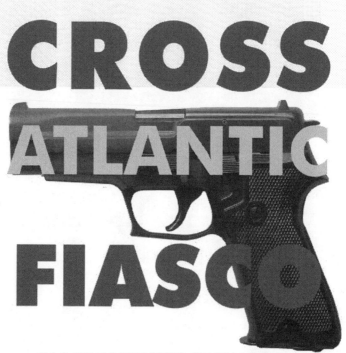

CROSS ATLANTIC FIASCO

BLOOD IS THICKER THAN WATER

JOHN A. ANDREWS

RENEGADE COPS

Creator of

The RUDE BUAY Series

&

The WHODUNIT CHRONICLES

RUDE BUAY ... SHATTERPROOF

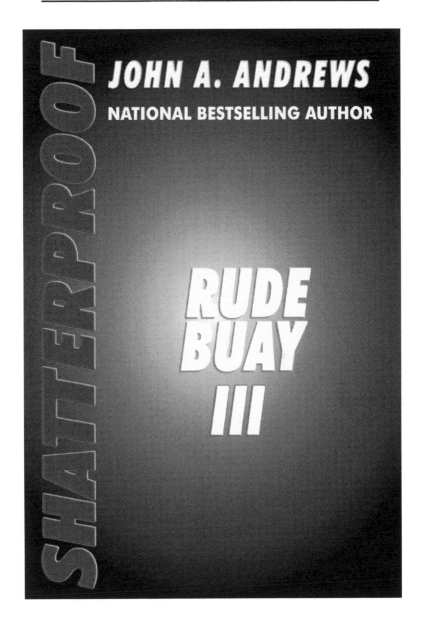

THE RUDE BUAY TRILOGY

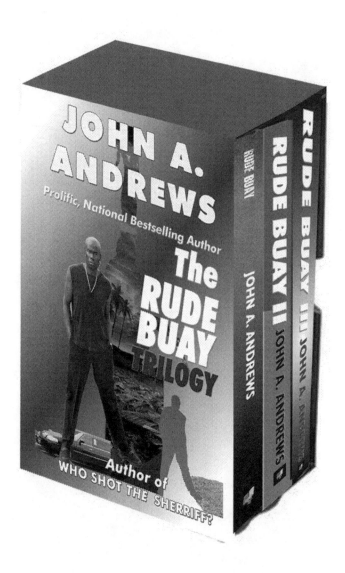

RUDE BUAY ... L'IRRESISTIBLE

<u>DON'T PLAY WITH MATCHES</u>

001 ... ONE MAN STANDING

OBJECTION OVERRULED!

John A. Andrews

TRUTH The WHOLE TRUTH ...

OBJECTION OVERRULED!

~The *WHODUNIT* CHRONICLES II~

By

Creator of
The RUDE BUAY Series®

National Bestselling Author

NEW RELEASES

RUDE BUAY ... THE UNTOUCHABLE

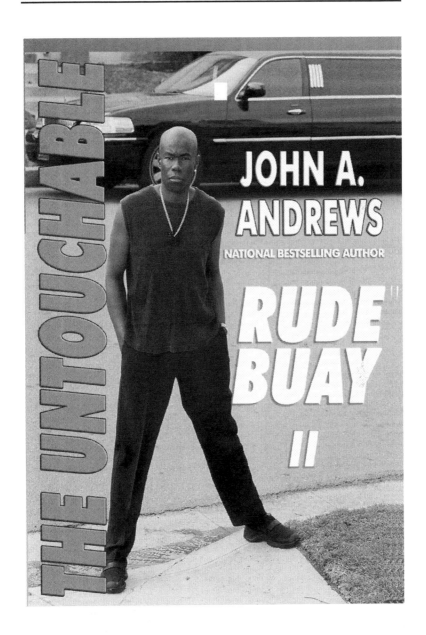

CHICO RUDO ... El INTOCABLE

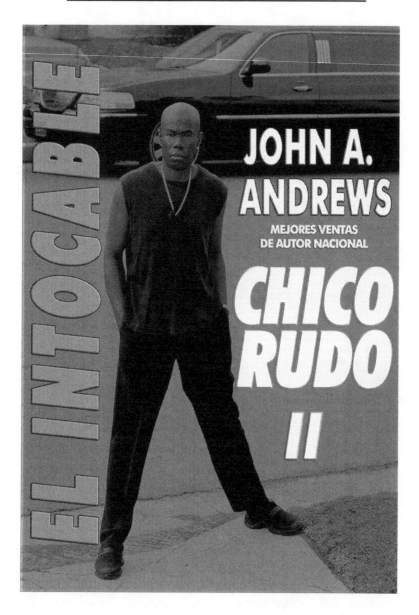

HOW I RAISED MYSELF FROM FAILURE TO SUCCESS IN HOLLYWOOD

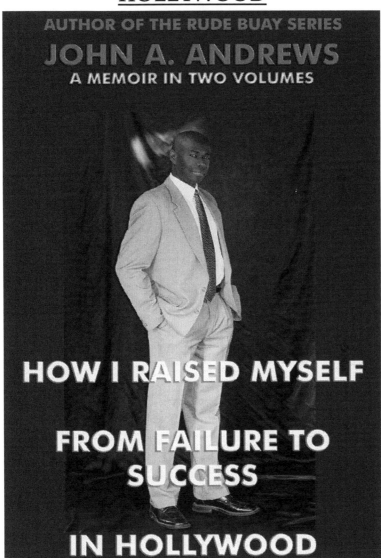

OTHER RELEASES
HOW I WROTE 8 BOOKS IN ONE YEAR

How I Wrote 8 Books In One Year

JOHN A. ANDREWS

A

Author of
TOTAL COMMITTMENT
The Mindset Of Champions

RUDE BUAY ... THE UNSTOPPABLE

QUOTES UNLIMITED II

DARE TO MAKE A DIFFERENCE – SUCCESS 101

National Bestselling Author

Dare To Make A Difference

SUCCESS 101

JOHN A. ANDREWS

QUOTES UNLIMITED

# WHO SHOT THE SHERRIFF?

THE 5 STEPS TO CHANGING YOUR LIFE

National Bestselling Author of
Rude Buay ... The Unstoppable

THE 5
STEPS TO
CHANGING
YOUR LIFE
BY: JOHN A. ANDREWS

DARE TO MAKE A DIFFERENCE - SUCCESS 101 FOR TEENS

THE 5 Ps FOR TEENS

SPREAD SOME LOVE – RELATIONSHIPS 101

TOTAL COMMITMENT

By National Bestselling Author of Rude Buay ... The Unstoppable

TOTAL COMMITMENT
The Mindset of Champions

JOHN A. ANDREWS

WHO SHOT THE SHERRIFF?

WHOSE WOMAN WAS SHE?

WHEN THE DUST SETTLES –
I AM STILL STANDING

CHICO RUDO ... EL IMPARABLE

RUDE BUAY ... THE UNSTOPPABLE
CHINESE EDITION

VISIT: WWW.JOHNAANDREWS.COM

www.WhodunitChronicles.com

Made in the USA
Charleston, SC
23 May 2014